"We were meeting Mama Llama," Isaac said.

Rebecca had to look at him, had to pretend that everything was just fine. She wasn't shaking on the inside, revisited by the past and memories that threatened everything.

"Mama Llama doesn't appear to like you very much," Rebecca said, pointing to the llama that had drawn back and now bared teeth at Isaac.

"Females sometimes take an instant dislike to me. I can't imagine why, when I'm always charming."

"He let me brush his horse," Allie chimed in. It seemed not all females disliked the cowboy.

"That must have been fun. And where is Eve?"

Allie shot Isaac a worried look and Rebecca pretended not to notice his wink.

"She had to get some work done," he supplied.

Not only had he charmed her daughter, now he was aiding and abetting her. Rebecca pinned him with a look and, like her daughter, he squirmed a little with guilt.

"And she brought Allie to you."

Allie groaned. "I might have sneaked off."

"Confession," Isaac said. "Always good for the soul."

Brenda Minton lives in the Ozarks with her husband, children, cats, dogs and strays. She is a pastor's wife, Sunday-school teacher, coffee addict and sleep deprived. Not in that order. Her dream to be an author for Harlequin started somewhere in the pages of a romance novel about a young American woman stranded in a Spanish castle. Her dreams came true, and twenty-plus books later, she is an author hoping to inspire young girls to dream.

Books by Brenda Minton

Love Inspired

Mercy Ranch

Reunited with the Rancher
The Rancher's Christmas Match

Bluebonnet Springs

Second Chance Rancher
The Rancher's Christmas Bride
The Rancher's Secret Child

Martin's Crossing

A Rancher for Christmas
The Rancher Takes a Bride
The Rancher's Second Chance
The Rancher's First Love
Her Rancher Bodyguard
Her Guardian Rancher

Visit the Author Profile page at Harlequin.com for more titles.

The Rancher's Christmas Match

Brenda Minton

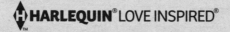

Recycling programs
for this product may
not exist in your area.

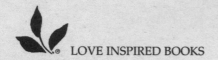

LOVE INSPIRED BOOKS

ISBN-13: 978-1-335-50991-8

The Rancher's Christmas Match

And suddenly there was with the angel a
multitude of the heavenly host praising God,
and saying, Glory to God in the highest,
and on earth peace, good will toward men.
—*Luke* 2:13–14

This book is dedicated to my friend Lori,
for all of her encouragement.

Chapter One

❧

Isaac West stood at the door of the feed store, letting his eyes adjust to the late November sunshine pouring down on Hope, Oklahoma. Some days a guy just preferred clouds. This happened to be one of them. The bright sunshine made his head spin and needlelike jabs of pain above his temple warned that a headache would knock him down before he could get back to the ranch.

It had been a good two months since he'd had the last headache. He'd kinda hoped he'd seen the last of them.

"Isaac, are you okay?" Mrs. Adams, the owner of the feed store, called out to him, her voice filtering through the long tunnel that had been his hearing for the past six years.

"I'm good."

"You're looking a little on the pale side. You want me to call Jack and have him pick you up?"

He didn't bother with denials. In a town the size of Hope, everyone knew everyone else's business. Mrs. Adams meant well. After all, as she liked to point out, she'd known him since he was knee-high to a grasshopper.

"Nah, I'm good," he assured her. "Right as rain."

He pulled a toothpick from his pocket and stuck it between his teeth. Might as well just get it over with. He pushed the door open and headed down the sidewalk in the direction of his truck. He stumbled a bit as he stepped down off the curb and lurched to the left, falling against a bright red sports car. The driver of that car slammed her door and glared at him.

He cringed a little. Partly from the madder-than-a-wet-hen look on her face, mostly because the slamming car door vibrated through his skull.

"What in the world is wrong with you?" She spoke with a sweeter-than-honey Oklahoma accent that matched her honey-blond hair and big brown eyes. But the spark in her voice said she was more than a little put out.

If it had been any other day, and if he'd been any other man, he would have flirted. Today wasn't a good day for being charming. He did try to tip his cowboy hat in a way that appeared chivalrous, when really, he just wanted to get home and away from everyone. Even pretty women.

"Sorry, ma'am, I lost my balance."

She came around the back of her little car and stepped in front of him, blocking the path to his truck. She was a head shorter than his almost six feet, and she was too thin. She was kind of pale, too. Like she didn't sleep much.

He shouldn't judge. It wasn't like he got a full eight hours every night. More like eight hours every two days. And a woman definitely didn't want someone pointing out that she needed a steak, mashed potatoes and more sleep.

At that moment she was surveying him with a less-than-appreciative gleam in her milk-chocolate brown eyes.

"Balance, my foot. Hand over your keys." She tipped her chin up. "I have a nine-year-old daughter, and the last thing I want is someone in your condition behind the wheel of a car. Or a truck."

He grinned a little and her eyes narrowed.

She extended her hand, nails manicured to perfection with the prettiest dark pink polish, and arched an eyebrow at his reluctance to hand over his keys. It took him at least five seconds to realize she thought he was drunk. He almost laughed. Almost.

She was pretty enough that he didn't mind the insult. After all, she had no way of knowing. People, he realized, saw what they wanted to see.

As it happened, she smelled like sunshine and he wouldn't mind a ride home.

"Stop grinning and say something!" she demanded. Most women waited until they'd known him at least a day or two before they reached that level of outrage.

The two of them were causing a scene. People were starting to stare. A few locals grinned and marched on by, willing to leave him to his fate. He pulled the keys out of his pocket and dropped them in her very lovely hand.

"Where do you live?" she demanded, a little less confident now that she had his keys. He figured she might be afraid.

"I'm not going to hurt you."

At his declaration she stepped back, and her throat bobbed as she swallowed a little bit of her outrage and dealt with her fear. If he had to guess, she wasn't usually the kind of woman who made impulsive decisions, and demanding his keys had been a rash one.

"Of course you won't," she stated. "I have a child in my car. I really do not want any trouble."

He noticed her lips were the same shade as her nail polish, and she bit down on the bottom one, her gaze darting about.

"Looking for a better option?" he asked. "I assure you there isn't a taxi or Uber in sight."

"Of course there isn't." She looked at the keys in her hand. "Get in my car."

He wanted to say a mighty loud, "Thank you, God." But he refrained. His head was killing him and he didn't really care what she thought of him. He slid into the passenger seat of the tin can she called a car and pulled his hat down over his eyes.

Miss Sunshine and Happiness got in on the driver's side. Man, she smelled good.

She said something, but since she was talking into his bad ear he didn't catch a word of it. He glanced her way, started to ask her to repeat, then noticed she really did have a child in the car. The little girl appeared to be nine or ten. She had wide brown eyes and the same honey-colored hair as her mother.

"Mom, didn't you say we never talk to strangers?" she asked, a cheeky grin on her face. He instantly liked the kid. She might be a replica of her mother, but there was a happy sparkle in her eyes. Life was still an adventure at that age.

He shifted his gaze from the girl to the woman in the driver's seat. The movement caused a sharp pain in the side of his head. At this point he usually had a cup of his sister-in-law Kylie's tea in hand as he crawled into a dark room.

"I said to buckle up," Miss Sunshine and Happiness said with a dose of aggravation, which meant she'd already said it once.

He guessed it was too late to explain that he wasn't intentionally ignoring her. He buckled up.

"Where do I take you?"

"Mercy Ranch."

"Mercy Ranch? The ranch owned by Jack West?"

"The same. Do you know where it is?"

"Yes, I have an appointment with Mr. West."

Interesting. She'd been on her way to the ranch. She didn't look like a veteran. Jack and his ranch for wounded warriors had become nationally known in the last couple years. But then, what did a wounded warrior look like? They weren't all men with big scars on the sides of their heads, or missing limbs. Some injuries were internal. Some were heart deep and resulted in nightmares and anxiety.

He was curious, but not curious enough to continue the conversation.

"Do you work at the ranch?" the child in the back seat asked.

It was difficult to hear when her voice had to compete with road noise, the whistle of wind battering the window of the car and the oldies station playing on the radio. Any other time he might have glanced back. At the moment, movement was not his friend and it was best to remain still, his head turned toward the driver.

As a matter of fact, his stomach was suddenly making him feel less than manly.

"My daughter asked you a question," Miss Happiness and Sunshine informed him.

"Yes." The one word came out a little curt. He could do better than that. "I work at the ranch."

"Are you going to be sick?" the child asked.

"Maybe," he muttered.

He thought of a scenario a little more to his liking, one in which he rescued this woman and showed her that a real man didn't need to be given a ride home, didn't need to be coddled and talked to like he was five. He had a feeling this woman, Miss Happiness and Sunshine, didn't like being rescued. She didn't strike him as a damsel in distress.

She probably slayed dragons and stormed castle walls. He could do those things on an average day. Unfortunately, today wasn't his best knight-in-shining-armor day.

The random thoughts worked, the way they sometimes did, to calm his brain and lessen the head pain. Not moving happened to be another key to ridding himself of the knife-sharp ache.

"You do look a little green," the woman said as she gave him a quick glance. What was her name? he wondered.

"Paula," he mumbled.

"What?"

"Trying to guess your name." He slid the hat back a fraction just so he could see her face. He caught what might have been the beginning of amusement hovering in her eyes. "Rachel?"

"No."

The child in the back seat laughed. The sound bounced around the vehicle. "Rebecca. Her name is Rebecca."

Isaac's eyes widened and he reached for the door. "Stop the car."

The woman quickly pulled to the shoulder and he practically fell as he escaped the car and stumbled to the ditch. He didn't lose his lunch, but came pretty close to losing his confidence.

Rebecca Barnes glanced at the driveway just fifty feet from where she'd pulled to the side of the road. They'd almost made it to Mercy Ranch. An arched entry with the name emblazoned in wrought iron, and an open gate, heralded their destination. But she couldn't consider herself arrived if she was standing on the side of the road. The cowboy she'd given a ride to stood in the ditch, bent over, trying to catch his breath.

"Do you think he's okay?" Allie asked from the back seat. She had raised herself up a bit to eye their passenger.

"Get your seat belt back on," Rebecca warned. But she watched closely, waiting to see if he would need help. She'd been chastising herself this entire time, because she'd gone and done it again. She'd been in Hope for less than an hour and she'd immediately bumped into what had to be the classic description of a bad boy. And she had a "no bad boys" policy. She didn't want trouble in her life, so she avoided men who appeared to be trouble, hinted at trouble or were confirmed trouble.

It was a fairly new motto, put in place when the latest disappointment, a friend, had exited her life with a large chunk of her business profits.

"He's fine," she answered her daughter. "Just a little under the weather."

"You think he's drunk," Allie stated, with a knowing tone to her voice.

"Allie, that isn't for you to say."

"I know, Mom." She now sounded contrite. Rebecca didn't have to look at her daughter to know the tone wouldn't match the look on her face.

Rebecca sighed and reached for the door. "I'm going to make sure he's okay, and then we'll head on to the ranch for the appointment with Mr. West. Are you okay?"

Allie nodded, but her attention was glued to the man in the ditch. He had straightened and now shifted his cowboy hat, wiping his brow with his arm. He glanced toward Rebecca as she got out of the car.

"Need help?" she asked.

"Nope." He trudged up the hill, slowly, but far more steady on his feet than he'd been when they first met.

Bad boy or not, he was easy on the eyes. Tall, just broad enough through the shoulders to think he'd be easy to lean on, and even in late November he'd held on to a golden tan. His hair was dark and his eyes were the gray of clouds bringing a winter storm.

She nearly sighed at her own ridiculous inventorying of his good looks. He was a cowboy. The kind that wore faded jeans and scuffed up boots. He was obviously trouble. And she needed to stay on task and not fall prey to anything or anyone that would distract her from her mission.

With Aunt Evelyn gone, Rebecca and Allie were the closest they'd ever been to being on their own. But they had each other, a nest egg to fall back on and a plan. Part of that plan included meeting with Jack West.

The cowboy had returned to the shoulder of the road

and he seemed a little more clear-eyed than he'd been a short time ago. A shaky hand brushed through his hair before he replaced his black cowboy hat, neatly hiding the scar that had drawn her attention. It snaked from the side of his face to the portion of his scalp just above his ear.

She guessed he was one of Jack West's veterans.

"Ready to go?" he asked, as he walked with her to the driver's side of the car. He opened her door and motioned for her to get behind the wheel.

"Yes. And thank you." She didn't know what else to say as he closed her door and headed back to the passenger side.

Moments later they were easing down the paved driveway of Mercy Ranch. It appeared to be a sprawling place, with rolling hills of winter-brown grass. White vinyl fencing split the land, creating corrals, smaller pastures, then wide-open fields. Her passenger pointed toward a large, log-sided home, but beyond that she saw an older white farmhouse, a metal building that appeared to be living quarters and, to the left, a large stable.

She parked next to the log house. The place glittered in the late-afternoon sun as the light reflected off the windows. A dog, a big yellow Labrador, lazed on the front porch.

"Here we are," he said. But he sat there a moment, not moving.

"Are you going to be sick again?" Allie asked from the back seat. "Does your head hurt? Is your vision blurry?"

"Allie," Rebecca warned.

He didn't seem offended. But he did turn and ask Allie to repeat what she'd said. She did and he smiled.

"I do have a headache and I'm not going to be sick. And my vision is just fine."

He got out of the car and said to Rebecca, "If you need to see Jack, I can get him for you. Oh, and I'll take my keys."

She handed him the keys she'd dropped in her purse. "I'm thirty minutes early."

"He won't mind that you're early." Isaac closed the door and walked away.

She hadn't planned on getting out, but the cowboy had stopped walking and leaned against the front of her car.

"I think he needs help, Mom," Allie piped up.

Rebecca closed her eyes and sent a rare petition for aid from above. "Come on, let's help him to the house and we'll see if Mr. West is available."

"Good!" Allie jumped from the car and hurried around to pet the dog that had meandered off the porch to greet them.

"Allie, you don't know the dog." Rebecca called out the warning, but it was too late. Allie had her arms around it and the animal didn't seem to mind.

"Decide to come on up to the house?" the cowboy asked.

"Allie thought you might need assistance."

"That's kind of her. It isn't usually this bad."

"Maybe you should see about getting help."

He didn't take her advice at all seriously. Instead, he leaned on her a bit.

She considered putting some distance between them,

but at that moment he stumbled. She put a steadying hand on his arm.

"If you can help me to the house, I'll get Jack for you."

They were halfway there when the door opened and a man stepped out on the porch. He looked like an older version of the cowboy, but broader through the shoulders, and his dark hair had grayed. At the sight of the two of them, he shook his head.

"Isaac, I've been wondering what kept you."

Isaac. She groaned, because now she understood his amusement with her name. Isaac and Rebecca, the Bible couple, parents of Jacob and Esau. She wanted no part of it. She didn't want to be a biblical reference.

"Dad, let me introduce you to Rebecca. She gave me a ride home when it appeared I might be intoxicated." He winked at her. "Rebecca, meet Jack West."

Jack stepped down off the porch, his left side trembling as he navigated the stairs. His arm jerked a bit and he said something under his breath. Even with his obvious physical problems, he appeared strong, and he smiled at her with all the charm she'd expected after reading articles about him and speaking with him on the phone.

"Miss Rebecca, I'm glad you're here. And that must be your little girl, Allie. I'll apologize for Isaac. He isn't as funny as he thinks he is. But he's most definitely sober."

With a tip of his hat, Isaac headed for the stairs. "Sorry to disappoint you, darlin', but I needed a ride home and your offer came at the right time. I'm going to leave you all to your meeting."

His gaze shot past her, to where Allie played with the yellow Labrador. His smile dissolved. "Maximus, stay."

His command caught Rebecca's attention and she turned to witness the dog leaning close to Allie as her daughter froze and then fell to the ground. As the seizure took control, Maximus stretched out beside her. Rebecca felt the world close in around her as she hurried to Allie, rolling her to her side. Allie's body jerked, and as the seizure continued, Rebecca glanced at her watch, timing the event.

Jack and Isaac had come over to sit next to her, and Isaac was on the phone.

Finally, the seizure ended and Allie lay motionless, her body curling in a fetal position as tears streamed down her cheeks. The dog licked her face and remained still, but near her side. Rebecca waited a moment, then gathered Allie in her arms.

"I'm sorry, Mr. West, this meeting was a bad idea. I can't do this." She blinked away tears that threatened to fall.

"Now, let's all stay calm." He had a hand on her shoulder, the way a father or grandfather would. She shut her eyes, wondering what that would feel like to have a father who cared.

"I called Carson, and he's on his way." Isaac West spoke, his voice steady. He was obviously sober. Sober, steady, calm. How had she missed that?

He stood up and held a hand out to his father. Jack clasped it readily and rose to his feet.

"Can we take her inside now?" Isaac asked.

Rebecca nodded and tried to stand, while still holding her daughter close. Isaac reached for her child, his gray eyes warm with sympathy. Without thinking, she tightened her hold. Allie whimpered in protest.

"I'm only going to carry her inside for you," Isaac offered.

Rebecca closed her eyes again, aware of the stillness all around her, the stillness of the child in her arms. Jack West's strong hand again settled on her shoulder as she remained on the grass, cradling Allie close.

"Let Isaac help you. We'll get you both inside and warmed up. My other son Carson is a doctor. He'll be here in just a few minutes to examine her."

She looked down at Allie. Slowly, she loosened her grip and Isaac took the child from her arms. Jack offered a surprisingly strong hand and pulled her to her feet.

The dog, Maximus, remained near Isaac, his intelligent eyes focused on Allie.

"He knew," Rebecca said, reaching a hand to the animal and letting him lick her fingers.

"He knew," Isaac said softly, a different version of the man she'd met in front of the store.

This version was a different kind of threat. His gaze rested on the little girl in his arms, concern shifting his features. Less than thirty minutes ago he had been having a hard time walking out of the local feed store. She tried to take her daughter from his arms.

"I can carry her," she said, as she reached for Allie.

"You help Jack and I'll manage," he said, winking at her.

"But you were just..." She was unsure how she should put this without hurting his feelings.

"I'm fine. The balance issues come and go."

She didn't know what to say, but she really didn't

have time to think about it. Allie had begun to cry as the effects of the seizure abated and she came back to herself a bit more.

"Trust me," he said.

Trust wasn't easy for Rebecca. Especially where Allie was concerned.

Life had proved to her that there were few people she could trust. There were few individuals she counted on. People had a tendency to let Rebecca and her daughter down.

That was her reality.

She'd come to Hope to create a new reality. She wanted Allie to have family in her life, people she could count on and a community she could grow up in. Since she had to start somewhere, she thought she might as well start by trusting this man.

Chapter Two

Isaac knew that life was all about choices. He'd made the choice to join the army, partly to serve his country and partly because he knew it would make Jack West, his father, madder than anything. He'd made a choice that morning to tease the pretty blonde who had assumed he'd been drinking.

The decision to join the military had changed his life. Forever. It had matured him, scarred him and left him with nightmares he wouldn't wish on anyone. Accepting the ride from Rebecca Barnes was not going to be one of those life-altering choices. It had only been a ride home, nothing more. As he entered the house carrying the little girl, Allie, he knew better than to fool himself into thinking Rebecca was a woman who wouldn't change a man's life. She had a past. It was written all over her face. It was the lack of trust in her eyes. It was the hesitant reply when Jack told her she could trust his son.

It was the little girl in his arms, no bigger than a minute and wearing a dazed look in eyes that matched her mother's.

She whimpered a bit and Rebecca immediately moved closer, bottom lip between her teeth as she studied her daughter.

"You're okay," she said. The words seemed to be as much for herself as for her child.

"I'm going to put her on the couch, and if you want, you can grab the quilt off the rocking chair to cover her." He smiled down at Allie. "You're okay. I know it always takes me a minute to get my bearings back when I have a spell."

Mischief lit the little girl's eyes. "Like when you got carsick."

He settled her on the leather sofa. "Grown men do not get carsick."

"You did," she said with a teasing tone. "But I won't tell."

"How much is it going to cost me?" he said, sitting on the coffee table not too far away from their young patient.

"Hmm," she said, closing her eyes. "I'll have to think about that."

Rebecca appeared at his side, quilt in hand. She smoothed it over her child and then leaned down to kiss Allie's forehead. "You're okay?"

"Mom…" the child pleaded. For normalcy, Isaac realized. She didn't want her health questioned. She wanted to run and play and didn't want people to watch, waiting for her to have another seizure.

The back door slammed and voices drifted to the living room. Carson had arrived. And with him, Kylie. She'd been a friend to Carson when the two were teens. She'd also been a wounded warrior living on the ranch when Carson returned a little over a year ago.

"That would be my brother, our resident doctor. He'll take good care of you." Isaac pushed himself to his feet and gave Rebecca more room to sit with her daughter.

"You're not leaving, are you?" Allie asked.

Huddled beneath the quilt, the little girl seemed smaller. But her eyes were bright and Isaac knew she'd be just fine. He also knew she needed Carson, not him. He needed to escape, because the last thing he wanted was for her to think he was the guy she should count on.

"I'm afraid I have to go," he told her. "I'm going to talk my sister-in-law into making me a cup of tea."

At that moment Kylie entered the room with her husband, Isaac's half brother. Her gaze darted from the child and her mother to Isaac. Carson took over and Isaac slipped from the room, aware of the mother in a way that he wished he wasn't. He was conscious of her fear for her daughter, and also that she smelled like something soft and floral. He'd been cognizant of her dislike for him and he'd known when that feeling had shifted just the smallest amount.

And all of that meant he needed to mind his own business and let the others tend to Rebecca and her daughter.

Kylie followed him to the kitchen, a large room that was the center of activity for the ranch house Jack had built ten years ago. The house stood as a testament to Jack's recovery. He'd conquered his past, overcome alcoholism and turned his life around in a way few people had expected.

Then he'd started Mercy Ranch, a place where wounded warriors could find a safe place to heal and start over. The mission and ministry had started when Jack picked Isaac up at a VA hospital. He'd looked around, seen people a lot like himself and realized he could do something for those having a hard time starting over.

The kitchen was blessedly dark, with just the dim lights over the sink for lighting. The headache appeared to be back in full force and the last thing Isaac wanted was to stand around in the sunny living room with a dozen people all talking at once.

Kylie moved quietly, scooping tea into a cup and setting a kettle on to boil. "The oil is in the cabinet," she told him.

Her special blend of oils, made for headaches. It wasn't a cure-all but it helped when nothing else would. He refused to continue taking prescription pain pills. He'd realized early on that genetics were a thing and he had a fear of turning into Jack. Or the man Jack had been, before conquering his addiction.

He poured a few drops of oil in his palm and applied it to his temples as he waited for the cup of tea to steep.

"How'd you find them?" Kylie asked.

"Find them?"

"The girl and her mother?" Kylie slid the tea across the counter to him.

"I was at the feed store, ordering grain, and she offered me a ride home." He shrugged, as if it hadn't been a big deal.

Kylie's eyes widened. "A woman with a little girl gave a random stranger a ride?" She leaned on the counter.

"Something like that," he offered.

"You're not that charming," she said.

"No, I'm not. She thought I'd been drinking and didn't want me driving."

Kylie chuckled. "That sounds more like it. And you were only too willing to take her up on the offer, huh?"

Isaac grabbed his cup, tipped his hat at his well-meaning sister-in-law and decided it was time to find a dark corner.

"I never took you for a coward," she called out to his retreating back.

"I never said otherwise," he called back to her without turning.

He pulled his sunglasses out of his pocket. With the shades in place, he headed out the back door and in the direction of the old farmhouse that Jack had remodeled for the men who called Mercy Ranch home.

The cool November air revived him a bit as he crossed the wide expanse of lawn in the direction of the two-story house that had been Jack's when Isaac first came to live here. Or more accurately, when his mother had dumped him here at the ranch. She'd told Jack that his son was getting difficult and she'd done her time as parent.

Done her time. As if parenting had been a prison for her.

In a way, he guessed it had. She'd had to occasionally think of someone other than herself. Which meant she'd kept a supply of soup in the cabinets and he'd fended for himself while she'd been off partying with friends.

In the beginning, life with Jack hadn't been much better. Isaac had been a rebellious preteen. Jack had been a raging, heavy on the rage, alcoholic.

Isaac sipped his tea as he walked, inhaling the bitter brew that tasted as bad as it smelled. As long as it helped the headache, he didn't mind.

Ted, the Australian shepherd he'd brought home

more than a dozen years ago, met him as he approached the house. The dog had slowed down a bit. Old age and a bad run-in with a car on the road had left the dog as gimpy as some of the men who lived at Mercy Ranch. But Ted was loyal and just about the best company Isaac knew of. As he climbed the back porch steps, he settled his hand on the dog's dark gray head.

"They're right about dogs being man's best friend, Ted. Don't let anyone tell you otherwise." He'd gotten the dog during his rougher-than-a-dirt-road teen years. The animal had been waiting for him when he returned from Afghanistan, wounded and angry.

"I guess that means I'm not your best friend?" Joe Lawson, another resident of the ranch, called out from the kitchen.

"You're a friend," Isaac responded. "But you're kind of worthless at arm wrestling and not much of a right-hand man."

"I never get tired of that joke," Joe grumbled, doing a decent job of fixing a pot of coffee with his left hand. He'd lost his right arm when an IED exploded in Kabul.

"I never get tired of saying it," Isaac responded. It was the same joke and the same comeback every day. Routine. They lived for routine.

They all had their stories. They didn't share much of their past or even much about what had brought them to Mercy Ranch. People called them wounded warriors but they were survivors.

"Going to bed?" Joe called out as Isaac headed for the stairs.

"Yeah."

"Bad?" the other man asked.

"Not the worst, but I'd like to head it off at the pass."

Joe came out from behind the counter, wiping his hand on the apron that hung from his neck. Joe found therapy in cooking.

"Eve said a woman brought you home. Her little girl had a seizure."

If there'd been a list of things, that subject would have come under the heading Last Thing in the World Isaac Wants to Discuss. But Joe knew that. And Joe didn't care.

"I'm going to my room. Make sure no one knocks on my door."

"Gotcha."

He pretended he didn't hear Joe's laughter following him up the stairs.

"She's fine," Dr. Carson West assured Rebecca as he sat back in the chair he'd pulled close to the sofa.

He winked at her daughter, who had his stethoscope in her ears, listening to her own heartbeat.

Of course Allie was fine. Rebecca drew in a deep breath at his reassurance. No matter how often this happened and how many times she heard that everything would be okay, it didn't get any easier. As a mother, she wanted to fix everything for her child. She wanted to take away the seizures, the fear, all of it.

"Has she always had them?" he asked, turning to face Rebecca.

"Five years."

"She could outgrow this," he offered.

"We hope she does. They've been happening less frequently."

"Only twice this year." Allie sat up a little, pulling

the stethoscope from around her neck and holding it out to Carson.

"How does it sound?" he asked.

"Like normal." Allie leaned back into the pillow and pulled the quilt up around her shoulders. "Where did Isaac go?"

Carson placed the stethoscope in his doctor bag. "He probably went to his room. When he has a headache, he's kind of a bear to be around."

"He carried me inside," Allie informed him. "He seemed nice. Even if my mom did think he had been—"

"That's enough," Rebecca held up a hand to cut her daughter off.

"I wouldn't suggest a long trip anytime soon," Carson said as he returned to the topic of Allie's health. "Let her rest up, and if you're staying in town, I'd like to see her in a couple of days."

"Thank you. I appreciate that."

Jack cleared his throat. "Where are you staying, Rebecca?"

She avoided his clear gray eyes, the eyes of a concerned parent. Why did that come to mind? And why did it bother her so much? She'd ceased missing her parents. She'd given up on any type of normal relationship with them. The last time she'd called her father, Pastor Don Barnes, he'd told her he didn't have a daughter.

Who was she kidding? His comment had hurt. It had opened up the wounds she'd buried at eighteen when he'd disowned her. It had ached deep down because he didn't want to meet his granddaughter.

And yet here she was, in Oklahoma and a short drive from where she'd grown up. Because even if family wanted nothing to do with her, she wanted to know they were nearby. If something happened, she wanted to know they had someone close.

She'd come to Hope to talk to Jack about the business opportunity he'd advertised nationally. Jack West was offering people free rent if they would commit to keeping their business in Hope, Oklahoma, for one year. But first he had to approve the business and the business plan.

"I thought we would have our meeting, and then I would drive to Tulsa and stay with a friend."

"We can discuss where you'll stay while we're going over your business plan," Jack continued. "We may need a few days to look over your business and I'm afraid the hotel in town is booked up. There's a festival in Grove and the entire area is overrun with visitors. Which we aren't going to complain about."

"I'll find us a place." She smiled, looking over at Allie.

Jack's attention slid to the girl and he winked at her. "I think you all should stay right here on the ranch."

"We couldn't," Rebecca replied. Allie loved animals and anything country. But they couldn't stay here.

"I don't see why not," Jack continued. "You have a briefcase that I'm sure contains a business plan. And I have a shop looking for a new owner. The only way I can connect you to that shop is if I have an opportunity to look at what you have in mind. If you need an opinion other than mine, that you need to stay put for a while, I think Carson has already given it."

"I don't want to take advantage of your generosity," she told him.

"I didn't mean to put you on the spot," Jack said

softly. "If staying here makes you feel uncomfortable I'm sure we can find somewhere else for you to stay."

She had to be a grown-up about this.

The dog, Maximus, pushed his golden head against her leg. She stroked the soft fur and found courage. But hadn't she been drawing on that same courage for the past year? The death of her aunt had been a difficult blow.

It had taken courage to sell their salon and leave Arizona. It had taken more courage to return to Oklahoma, where she knew she'd meet her past head-on.

For Allie's sake she needed to make this work. For Allie she would do whatever it took. With that in mind she lifted her gaze to find Jack West watching her, his expression kind. She nodded, accepting the offer. "We'll stay."

Allie let out a weak shout and the dog quickly returned to her side, snuggling against her, his head resting on her shoulder. She ran a hand down his back and the dog pushed even closer.

"But we don't want to put you to any trouble," Rebecca added.

Jack waved off her concerns. "We have plenty of space. There's a nice couple of rooms in the women's dorm."

Kylie West came in the room and laughed. "'Women's dorm' is a fancy way of saying that there's a garage that's been remodeled and turned into apartments."

"Nice apartments," Jack countered.

Kylie inclined her head. "I'll agree with that. I lived in one of those apartments for several years."

"You don't live here?" Rebecca asked.

"Carson and I built a house just down the road."

Kylie pulled a chair close to Rebecca's. "There are a dozen people living on this ranch, plus family. I promise you won't be an imposition. And it looks like Maximus is begging your little girl to stick around."

"Thank you," she said to Jack. "I really do appreciate this. And thank you, Dr. West, for coming over here."

"Please, call me Carson. And if you have luggage, I'll help get you moved to your rooms."

Jack's head jerked a bit as he nodded, but his smile remained bright. "And if Kylie doesn't mind, she can take you on out to the garage and introduce you to the other ladies."

Moments later, Kylie led Rebecca and Allie out the back door of the ranch house and across the lawn to a garage turned living quarters for the three women who lived on the ranch. There was nothing garage-like about the structure, Rebecca realized. The garage doors had been removed and the building included a covered patio.

Inside, it appeared that Jack West had designed the building with a purpose. The doors were wide, for wheelchairs, the floors were hardwood, the furniture sparse with plenty of room for easy access to the living areas and kitchen.

For the next few days they would call this place home. Allie had already hurried to the windows that overlooked stables and fields. Rebecca sighed because she knew that in three days it would be difficult to tear her daughter away from Mercy Ranch.

And it wasn't just the ranch that would make Allie want to stay, it was the people. Especially a slightly off-balance cowboy with an easy smile and gray eyes that hinted at pain.

Chapter Three

Isaac ran a brush down the horse's side as Ted, the Australian shepherd, snoozed on a bale of hay. Shorty stomped when the brush hit a ticklish spot. Isaac moved the brush to the animal's back. He didn't normally get distracted when taking care of livestock. Clearly, he knew better than to daydream while working with a horse. Even a horse like Shorty that he'd spent a good amount of time with. In the business world, Shorty would have been his partner. They'd moved a lot of cattle together, he and Shorty. They'd spent long days riding fences, doing repairs, and they'd even won a few events in cutting horse competitions.

But he was distracted. Because he'd woken up this morning to the memory of Rebecca Barnes and her daughter. He'd actually smiled as he made his morning eggs and toast. Because she'd been unexpected and had a streak of courage that he guessed most people overlooked.

Some would have called it foolishness, to approach a stranger, ask for his keys and then offer him a ride home. If he ever saw her again he'd warn her not to do that. She was fortunate that he really was just a guy needing a ride home.

If Jack gave her a building, Isaac guessed he would be seeing her again. She'd be in town, maybe around the ranch. They would be in one another's lives.

"Is the horse ticklish?" a small voice asked from behind him.

He nearly jumped out of his skin. A grown man wouldn't want to admit that to just anyone, but considering that whoever had said it giggled at his reaction, he wouldn't stand a chance at denying. Doing his best to appear composed and tamping down the grin that tugged at his mouth, he faced the girl, who stood inside an empty stall, a scrawny, gray tabby kitten in her hands.

"Yep, horses are ticklish." He pushed his hat back to get a better look at her. "You feeling up to snuff today?"

"I don't know what that means, but I think it means I'm good. I always am. After." Her lips drew in as she contemplated him. "Are *you* up to snuff?"

He laughed. "Yeah, I am."

"Your dad says you sleep off the headaches. Does that help?"

She had a lot of questions for a little girl. The questions were bigger than she was, but he guessed with her seizures she had a maturity most nine-year-olds didn't possess.

"Yeah, it helps. I drink tea and I sleep. Usually when I wake up I'm better."

"Is it because of the scar on your head?"

There was no easy way to dodge these questions and no telling when she'd stop asking them.

"Yes, it's because of the scar."

"I don't have any scars. My mom says sometimes kids just have seizures. And I might outgrow it."

"That would be good."

"Will you outgrow your headaches?" she asked, completely serious.

"I might. Does your mom know you're out here?"

She shook her head and held tight to the kitten, which decided it might be time to make a break for it. "Did I ask too many questions? My mom says I'm nosy. I don't think I am. I just like to know stuff, and you can't know if you don't ask."

"I guess you have a good point." He gestured at the tabby, which had started to yowl. "You might want to let that kitten go before you get scratched," he warned.

The kitten jumped free and scampered sideways out of the stall, hissing as it ran for cover at the other end of the stable. Allie stepped out in turn and watched it make its escape.

"I was going to name him Stripe." She let out a big sigh.

"I'm sure he won't mind a name."

She frowned. "Yeah, but now he's gone. I've never had a cat before. We couldn't have pets at our apartment in Arizona."

He beat down the desire to ask his own questions. Questions were dangerous. Because they resulted in answers and that meant knowing a little too much about people.

The young person standing in front of him seemed to be making a valiant attempt to fight tears. If she hadn't looked sad he wouldn't have handed her the horse brush. As much as he didn't consider himself to be a kid person, he'd kind of grown fond of smaller humans since

Carson had shown up with his two. Maggie and Andy were as cute as two kids could be. This one seemed the same. She was smart and funny, and when a tear trickled down her cheek she dashed it away with an aggravated flick of a finger.

"How about brushing Shorty for me?" he offered.

She looked at the brush and looked at the sixteen-hand Quarter Horse. She didn't seem quite as sure of herself as she had when she first peeked up over the stall door.

"So where's your mom?" he asked as he grabbed a step stool and lifted her to stand on it. She looked unsure, so he guided her hand to brush the horse's neck.

As she brushed Shorty, Isaac glanced toward the double-door entrance to the stable. No sign of anyone looking for a runaway kid.

"She's meeting with Mr. West. That's your dad," she informed him.

He chuckled and she kept brushing.

"Did you stay in town last night?" he asked. He hated that he was so curious. But there was something about Rebecca Barnes. She was a mix of strength and sweetness, and then there was that slightly wounded and not-so-trusting glint in her eye.

Someone had hurt her. Maybe more than one someone.

He shook off the questions that he considered asking the little girl, who was busy brushing his horse, talking to it as if they were sharing their best-kept secrets.

"Nope." Allie handed him the brush. "We stayed here."

"Here?"

She gave him a curious look. "Are you going to be sick again?"

"I wasn't sick," he insisted. "And no, I'm not. I'm just surprised. I didn't know you stayed here."

"Because you were sleeping," she said, sounding matter-of-fact. "We had dinner with Jack. He told us Maria made the casserole. It was better than anything my mom can cook. She burns stuff. She says it's because she's distracted."

"She wouldn't want you telling everyone that she can't cook," he warned.

"You're not everyone. Anyway, we stayed here. In the garage. It's a nice garage with no cars in it, so I don't know why it's called a garage."

They'd stayed on the ranch. The thought unsettled him.

How much could he or should he ask without seeming too curious? He felt like a sixteen-year-old with a crush on the new girl. That wasn't happening. No way. No how.

"Hey!" A shout from the front of the stable caught his attention.

"Hey back," he returned.

Eve, a resident of the ranch, glared at him, then managed to soften her expression as she approached. Smile or no, she didn't appear to be too happy, and it seemed his pint-size stable hand might be the reason.

"You ran off." Eve pointed at the girl. "And you didn't ask permission or tell me where you were going. That really isn't very nice."

"Eve," he warned.

If there was another person on the ranch not naturally kid friendly, it was Eve. She'd come around by degrees as she'd gotten attached to Carson's children. But she would be the first to admit that she didn't have a lot of experience with children. She'd been an only child to what she referred to as her "hippy parents."

He wanted to laugh, because somehow she always got stuck babysitting.

"Do I look like a day-care provider?" she asked him.

"You seemed to do a pretty good job," Isaac teased. "Except you have a tendency to lose children. That can't be good."

"I wanted to see the horses," Allie explained. "I should have told you, but I thought you'd say no."

Eve maneuvered her chair around the horse, giving the animal a less-than-trusting glance. Shorty didn't even twitch.

"What if something had happened?" Eve asked the little girl.

Allie's shoulders hunkered forward and she sighed. "I didn't think about that. I just wanted to see the animals. Did you know there's a llama?"

Eve melted. She could act tough but on the inside she was a marshmallow. "Yeah, I know there's a llama. Do me a favor—next time ask. And if you're going to wander, take Maximus. Now we need to head back to the house. Your mom will be finished talking with Jack and she'll be looking for you."

"Do we have time to see the llama?" Allie moved close to Eve's chair and leaned on the armrest.

"I think so. But I don't do well in the dirt out there, so Isaac will have to take you." Eve shot him a look.

He glared back, the way he would have done if he'd had a little sister that pestered him. He did have a little sister, a half sister named Daisy. But since they'd never met, he didn't know if she was a pest.

"I'm kind of busy."

Eve smirked. "Doing what?"

He glanced down at Allie. "Work."

"What work would that be?" Eve continued.

"Believe it or not, Eve, ranch work is real work. There are fences to fix, cattle to work, horses we're training."

She saluted. "Gotcha, Sarge."

He held a hand out to the child at his side. "Even a spitting llama is better than a stubborn female."

As he walked away, Allie's hand in his, Eve called out, "When you get done, could you take her to the house? I have to get some work done."

"No problem," he called back to her.

Allie was silent for a minute. "Isn't she your friend?"

He glanced down at the blond-haired child. "She is my friend."

"Did you date and get mad at each other?"

"No, we just like to tease. She knows how to…" He cut off the explanation because a kid wouldn't understand Eve getting under his skin the way she did. "We just like to give each other a hard time. But no, we haven't dated. We're just friends."

Neither of them dated. It was the code on the ranch. This was a place for healing, for getting lives back in order. Relationships were unnecessary baggage for people dealing with physical and emotional problems they'd brought back from war.

The last thing he needed was to drag a woman into his messed-up life. He remembered all too well what it had been like living on this ranch with Jack, back when he was still fighting the nightmares of Vietnam. He remembered Jack climbing into the bottle and not climbing out for weeks, the ranch crumbling around his ears and livestock begging to be fed.

He wasn't Jack, but he feared the what-ifs.

What if he became Jack? What if he hurt a woman and children the way Jack had hurt his wife and kids?

Nah, it wasn't worth that kind of guilt. And fortunately there'd never been a woman who had made him consider getting serious.

The room Jack West used as an office was on a back corner of the sprawling log home. Massive windows offered a view of the wide-open fields belonging to the ranch. One wall of the room was lined with floor-to-ceiling bookcases. The shelves were filled with books and family pictures, as well as trophies the ranch had won at different rodeo events in the tristate area. Tristate meaning Oklahoma, Arkansas and Missouri.

Jack had explained it all at the beginning of the meeting. He'd shared personal details that had been uncomfortable to hear. Stories of his wife, his children, his road to recovery and, now, today, trying to forge a relationship with his estranged, adult children.

So far Carson was the only one of the three who had agreed to meet with him. Isaac was not a full brother to Carson and his siblings, Colt and Daisy.

"I'd love to show you the building I have available," Jack told Rebecca. "I think a salon with the potential to expand to a day spa is a terrific idea. I could see how it would benefit the resort we're renovating. Now I admit, I'm concerned with your ability to bring in local traffic."

"I think you might be surprised," she countered. "Also, we could advertise in nearby communities, like Grove. If people want to get away for the day, go to a top-notch salon, perhaps eat at the tearoom you say is going to be opening in the spring, then why not come to Hope?"

"Why not come to Hope?" He grinned at that. "Good point. We should use that in advertising to local communities."

She couldn't help but smile at his approval. Goodness, she had to stop needing this man's approval and she had to stop basking in his praise. He wasn't her father. And if he learned about her past, he might not be as easygoing as he appeared.

"Yes, why not come to Hope?" Rebecca repeated.

Jack gave her a long look. "Why did *you* come to Hope, Rebecca?"

The question took her by surprise. What should she tell him? She had a feeling he would find out her secrets somehow, some way.

"My parents live in Grove. After my aunt passed away last year, I realized Allie and I were adrift in Arizona with no support system. I had friends, but they were busy with their own lives. I decided to move closer to home and I saw your advertisement. My parents…" They wanted nothing to do with her or with Allie. But that didn't matter. If something happened to Rebecca, her parents would be there for Allie. She had to believe that. After all, she was their only child. Allie their only grandchild.

"Rebecca?"

She shook her head at the question. "I'm sorry, I got lost in thought."

"If you ever want to talk…" he offered. And then he grinned. "If you ever want to talk, Kylie is a good listener. I give too much advice and have too many opinions. Or at least that's what the folks hereabouts like to say."

"I'll keep that in mind." She glanced out the window, gathering thoughts that continued to go astray.

Thoughts that could get a woman in trouble. Thoughts of a cowboy with steel-gray eyes and a smile that flashed often and with a ton of mischievous charm. He'd disappeared yesterday after Allie's seizure and she hadn't seen him since. Not even when several of the ranch residents had gathered for dinner in the big dining room that connected to the kitchen.

No one had mentioned him. No one said anything about checking on him to make sure he was okay. Not that it mattered to her.

Her focus needed to stay on taking care of Allie and providing for them as best she could. She was a single mom with only herself to rely on. And now, strangely, she seemed to have a friend in Jack West. With that in mind, she had to do her best. She had to make a success of this salon.

Another quick glance out the window and the object of her thoughts appeared. And next to him, her daughter. They were standing at the fence, and Allie had climbed the bottom rail to stand next to him, her hand reaching for the white-and-black animal.

Rebecca stood. "I should go get Allie. I didn't mean to impose on Eve. And now it seems Isaac has taken over babysitting duty."

She diverted her attention back to Jack, who remained sitting in his deeply cushioned office chair.

He, too, had spotted Isaac and Allie, but didn't look concerned.

"She might have had to get some work done," he said of Eve, who had been a longtime resident of the ranch. "I'm afraid I hadn't planned on our meeting taking quite this long. And I apologize to you for that. Why don't you head on out there and make sure things are okay? Later we'll drive to town and take a look at the building. I'd like for you to see it in person and then we can compare your design ideas to the actual structure. If you like it, it's all yours."

"Thank you, Mr. West."

"Jack." He smiled as he corrected her.

"Thank you, Jack."

A moment later she was cutting across the lawn in the direction of the small enclosure where her daughter remained next to Isaac, her hand reaching for the llama, which seemed less interested in the grass in Allie's hand and more interested in the man next to her.

The llama must be female. He probably charmed all females, young children, animals. Not Rebecca, of course. She couldn't be charmed. She had no desire to be charmed. Ever again. Because charming men usually had an agenda and it usually ended with her being hurt.

"Hey," Rebecca called out. Allie glanced her way. Isaac continued to stare straight ahead. Ignoring her, of course.

The phone in her back pocket buzzed. She wanted to ignore it, but pulled it from her pocket and answered.

"Rebecca Barnes?" The voice wasn't a familiar one. It had been years, but her first thought was that something had happened to her parents.

"This is she."

"My name is Jared Owens. I'm a parole officer out of Springfield, Missouri."

Her heart dropped. This call could go only one way. It would bring back the past. It would bring back the guilt and the pain.

"Okay." She focused on Allie, who had turned around to watch her. Rebecca waved and smiled, as if the call hadn't left her cold inside.

"Miss Barnes, Greg Baxter was released from prison one month ago. He's missed two appointments with me and I have reason to believe he might be in Oklahoma."

"How did you get my number?" She hadn't been in contact with Greg in years. Not since he robbed a store, shortly after she'd realized she was pregnant with Allie. She'd been eighteen at the time and Greg had been a mistake. Her attention remained on Allie, who was definitely not a mistake. She was something beautiful from something so ugly and hurtful. Her daughter.

"Your mother gave me your number," he continued. "Miss Barnes, we have reason to believe that Greg will try to locate you and his daughter."

"No." The one word emerged from deep within. "He can't see her."

"I understand that. I agree that he should not be in your lives. I want you to understand that there is a warrant out for his arrest. He violated the conditions of his parole and it's our intention to bring him back to the state of Missouri. This is a courtesy call because I wouldn't want you to be taken by surprise should he try to contact you."

"Thank you. I do appreciate that."

"Miss Barnes, if he does contact you, please phone us. I'll give you my direct line."

"I'll put it in my phone." She managed to minimize the screen and switch to Contacts. With fingers that felt cold and clumsy she entered the name and number. The call ended. Her world shifted precariously as she considered what it meant to her life, to Allie's life, that Greg Baxter had been released. She drew in a deep breath and then exhaled. She wouldn't let him take anything else from her.

Over the years people had told her to have faith, to realize God had a plan. She'd been unable to find faith since the day her dad had told her that Allie's seizures were a direct result of Rebecca's sins.

"Mom?" Allie called out, her happy grin faltering.

Rebecca hurried forward, plastering a smile on her face and avoiding eye contact with the man who studied her with a knowing expression.

"We were meeting Mama Llama," he finally said.

She had to look at him, had to pretend that everything was just fine. Had to prove she wasn't shaking inside, threatened by the past and the memories.

"Mama Llama doesn't appear to like you very much," Rebecca said, pointing to the animal, which had drawn back and bared its teeth at Isaac.

"Yeah, females sometimes take an instant dislike to me. I can't imagine why."

"He let me brush his horse," Allie chimed in. It seemed not all females disliked the cowboy.

"That must have been fun. And where is Eve?"

Allie shot Isaac a worried look and Rebecca pretended not to notice his wink.

"She had to get some work done," he explained.

Not only had he charmed her daughter, now he was aiding and abetting her. Rebecca pinned him with a look, and like her daughter, he squirmed a little with guilt.

"And she brought Allie to you?"

Allie groaned. "I might have sneaked off while she was on the phone. I saw the horses."

"Telling the truth," Isaac said. "Always good for the soul."

Rebecca held out a hand to her daughter. "We're going to town for lunch and then we will meet Mr. West at the shop. Isaac, thank you."

He pushed against the llama as it reached across the fence to nip at his sleeve. The animal came back and grabbed his hat. Allie laughed until tears rolled down her cheeks, and the tension inside Rebecca eased.

Isaac pointed at Rebecca. "Was that a giggle, Ms. Barnes?"

"I'm an adult. I don't giggle." Rebecca smiled as he pushed his hat, tooth marks and all, back on his head.

"It most definitely was a giggle. And for that, I'm buying lunch."

Rebecca tried to object. She seriously wanted to tell him he couldn't. But before she could respond, Allie had jumped down off the railing, a huge grin on her face, obviously thrilled with the idea.

So she accepted. For Allie's sake. Nothing else.

Chapter Four

It didn't take a genius to see that Rebecca Barnes had secrets, and she guarded them as carefully as she did her daughter. Isaac liked that about her, even if it made it difficult to get to know her. Of course, he probably wasn't the easiest guy in the world to get to know.

He had his own closely guarded secrets and memories. He had plenty of things he didn't talk about.

As he contemplated her across the table from him, he thought about telling her he understood. He doubted this was the right time. Allie had been questioning her nonstop about Christmas. Once she'd mentioned grandparents, Rebecca had shot her a quick look to quiet her. Jack had noticed, as well as Kylie and Jack.

The five of them were having lunch at Mattie's Café in town. The proprietor, Holly Jones, had just made it around to their table, passing out samples of a new dessert she'd just invented.

"We need Christmas trees," Kylie mentioned casually, as she took a bite of the dessert. Her face puckered up and she blinked a few times.

Isaac laughed and Allie hid a giggle behind her hand.

He winked at the little girl and they waited as Kylie tried to get her face straight again, smiling across the café at Holly.

"You know she can't bake a cake," Isaac whispered. "Didn't you notice, I put all of mine on Rebecca's plate?"

Rebecca glanced down at it and her mouth dropped.

Isaac took his sister-in-law's plate and scraped the remaining cake onto Allie's. "Holly can't bake. She thinks she can. She watches those reality cooking shows where they make them put together horrible concoctions like salmon and chocolate. For some reason she probably thought anchovies would make a great dessert. A little lemon, some fish, a dash of poppy seeds."

"I heard that, Isaac West," Holly called out from across the room. "You're a horrible person."

"Holly Jones, you're going to jail for trying to poison the good citizens of Hope. There's no hope for your cakes."

Allie dissolved in giggles and even Rebecca forgot herself and laughed. Isaac caught himself staring at her. She glowed when she laughed. Her eyes lit up and her smile changed the casual beauty of her face into something extraordinary. If he lived to be one hundred, he would never forget that smile. Kylie elbowed him and he gulped and reached for water. Holly was crossing the room, her brown hair framing her elfin face. Her green eyes flashed with fire. She picked up the plate of cake and placed it in front of Isaac.

"I apologize, Kylie, your lunch is on me. You mistakenly got the cake I intended for Isaac."

All around them chuckles and laughter filled the café as people realized the joke had been on Isaac. Rebecca took a bite of her cake and smiled at him. "Mmm, delicious," she said.

"Holly, that just isn't Christian of you," Isaac said as he scooped up a bite of the cake he'd put in front of Rebecca. "This is actually edible. It really is lemon. And no anchovies."

"Fool. It's lemon and raspberry. I'm tired of you complaining about my inventions."

"Well, some of them just aren't that good," Isaac told her.

She wrinkled her nose at him, and then smiled at Allie. "I bet you'll be starting school here, won't you?"

Allie nodded. "Next week."

"You'll make a lot of very good friends. There are quite a few about your age in my Sunday school class. We're getting ready to start practicing for our Christmas play." She picked up an empty plate as she spoke. "I have to get back to work. You all have a good weekend. See you at church Sunday."

"Yeah, and I'll pray for you," Isaac called out to her retreating back.

"You do that, Isaac."

"We don't go to church," Allie said, to no one in particular. But Isaac noticed Rebecca's cheeks go slightly pink at her daughter's revelation.

"How about those Christmas trees," he interjected. "I love a big old Christmas tree. Especially cedar."

"Because you know I'm allergic," Jack grumbled. "We can pick up live trees at the feed store. They're in pots and we can plant them after Christmas."

"But we'll put the artificial tree in the main house," Kylie added. "The trees at the feed store are pretty, but they're never large enough for the living area."

Isaac agreed, but his gaze slid to the woman sitting across from him. Rebecca had a lost look on her face. It had started with the topic of church and hadn't gotten better when they'd switched to talking about Christmas trees.

She had stories, a troubled past. Right now she had a softness about her that hinted at tears. Not his problem.

He usually stuck to that motto, but Rebecca changed things. Because she didn't seek attention. She didn't put her pain out there for everyone to take a look at. She was private, strong and hurting.

He respected that.

He also liked her daughter, and he couldn't get that sad little voice out of his head when she'd said she didn't go to church. He remembered being about her age listening to other people talk about the things they did as families, things he never understood. Going to church together was one of the biggies. But there had been other things, like family dinners, trips to the lake, playing ball. A kid shouldn't have to yearn for the things that childhood seemed to guarantee.

With that in mind he spoke up. "About that Christmas program?" he said to Allie.

The little girl lit up and her mother's eyes narrowed. "I bet you'd love to be a part of it, wouldn't you?" he asked Allie. "If your mom doesn't mind. Every child gets a part and even if something goes wrong, it's still the best thing ever."

"I don't think so," Rebecca said.

At the same time Allie asked, "Do you think I could?"

Rebecca mouthed the word *don't* silently.

He got the message loud and clear.

Someone in church had hurt her. If he had to guess, it probably had something to do with Allie.

Jack got to his feet, steadier today. "We should get on the road. Rebecca is going to make a list of materials she'd like to purchase for the shop. Isaac, you should see to those Christmas trees."

Isaac grabbed the bill Holly had left on the table. "I'll do that, but I'd prefer to wait until Allie can go with me. I have a feeling she's a Christmas tree expert."

Just like he was an expert at getting involved where he shouldn't. Allie didn't remind him of a child in Afghanistan, a little girl with dark hair and pleading eyes. He'd seen her look his way. And then she'd been engulfed by the explosion, the smoke, the violence. Her story never made it to the news. No one thought about her or the tragedy of a young life lost. He remembered. His friends remembered. The image had stayed with them. There were times late at night that he'd get a text from one of the men he'd been stationed with, asking if he still had nightmares.

He did.

"Isaac." Jack's voice caught him mid-thought. A hand on his arm brought him back to the present and he managed to breathe, to clear his head. He swiped an arm across his forehead and walked off, still holding the bill for their lunch.

He heard Holly say something like "don't worry about it, it's on the house." Jack told her to take the money. Conversation buzzed around him as he walked out of the café, the door closing behind him, cutting him off from the buzz of curious voices.

As he walked down the sidewalk, a headache started. Throbbing pain began at his temple and radiated down to his ear and above his eye. He leaned against the building, closing his eyes as he drew in fresh air.

"Breathe," a low voice told him. He'd expected it to be Kylie. It wasn't, though. He was surprised to hear Rebecca's soft alto.

"Easier said than done." He opened his eyes, but squinted against the sun. He pulled sunglasses out of his pocket and slid them on.

She stood next to him, shoulder to shoulder. She was a surprise. First, he'd expected her to walk on, or to take the same stand she'd taken on Monday when she'd offered him a ride.

Instead, she remained next to him.

He matched his breathing to hers until his thoughts became rational once more. The sky was blue. A cool north wind brought the fragrant hint of fall turning to winter. The town maintenance crew was working from bucket trucks, hanging lights from poles.

His world was far removed from the terrors of Afghanistan. And yet he thought of all the children living in that country, listening at night for the sound of gunfire or bombs, wondering when a neighbor would be revealed as an enemy.

"Better?" she asked.

"Yeah, thanks."

She stepped away from the side of the building. "We all have our pasts to deal with. Things that might not be frightening to one person can be a nightmare to another."

"Church?" he asked, as she started to walk away.

Without looking back, she nodded. And he let her go, watching as she returned to her daughter. Allie grabbed her hand, said something that brought a frown to Rebecca's face, then they moved on.

He would follow. Soon.

The future home of the Hope Lakeside Salon was on a corner of Lakeside Drive just a block from Mattie's Café. The street was lined with brick-and-wood-sided buildings. The structure was two stories. Downstairs would house the salon, while the upstairs rooms were being remodeled to rent by the night.

Rebecca found herself overwhelmed and excited as she looked around. The building had been renovated, the walls painted ivory, leaving whoever started a business there to choose their own colors. There were several rooms, including a large main one that might have once been a store. A door led to a hallway and several smaller ones that would make treatment rooms as she expanded her business to include a day spa, offering facials and massages.

"This was a dry goods store when I was a kid growing up in town," Jack told her. "My mom would bring me here to buy shoes. She would buy cloth for sewing."

"Those are good memories," Rebecca agreed.

She had memories, too. Of gardening with her mother, helping her father clean the church. But senior year of high school everything had changed. She'd met Greg. And she'd learned that her father preached forgiveness to his congregation, but his daughter was exempt from his mercy.

The bell over the shop's door chimed. Isaac entered, looking more himself. He pushed his hat back and glanced around the bright, clean room.

"Will this building have the water you need for a salon?" he asked.

"I'll see that it does," Jack responded. He headed to the back corner of the room. "There's a restroom behind here, with water pipes. We'll have to run lines along this inside wall."

"I'm hoping to have four stations, for four stylists. I know that sounds ambitious," Rebecca said.

Isaac glanced around the store. The front had floor-to-ceiling windows, with an area to the right of the door where hair product displays might be located. The other exterior wall had two large windows that overlooked the lake, a short distance away.

"I think it's good to be ambitious," Jack told her. "I'll have them install five. Why not dream big. And what else will you have in this front area?"

"I think a couple of stations for manicures and pedicures, and possibly a small boutique in the back corner. Of course, it's going to happen in stages. I have the money to get the salon started. I'll need chairs, sinks, equipment."

"This is why I picked you, Rebecca." Jack sat on a folding chair in the corner. "I like that you're ambitious, but you know how to take things in stages."

She stood in the center of the room, picturing it all in her mind. Her dream. She wanted this, for herself and for her daughter. They would have stability here. They might still be two against the world, but the world around them would be smaller and they would at least feel less alone.

She didn't allow herself to think about having people to depend on. She'd believed she had that in Arizona and she'd been fooled. She'd made the disastrous choice to trust Robert Larkin as a business partner. She'd never expected the longtime friend of her aunt to embezzle money from the salon and disappear. His crime had become her failure. This time she wouldn't lose. She wouldn't let herself or Allie down.

"You okay?" Isaac asked. He hadn't sneaked up on her and yet his presence at her side took her by surprise. She smiled at him, noticing again the scar that zigzagged along his cheek and ended somewhere beneath the black cowboy hat.

"I'm good. Just daydreaming."

"Was it a nightmare? You looked pretty intense." He said it with a teasing grin that revealed a dimple in his right cheek.

"No, just a thought," she said as she walked away. His hand caught hold of her arm.

Still grasping her arm, he stepped in front of her. His carefree look had disappeared and those steel-gray eyes held her captive. She watched the slow flick of dark lashes over them, and drew in a breath.

"Since we're going to be around each other, you might need to know that I'm deaf in my left ear. I don't want you to think I'm walking off without answering you."

"Oh, I'm sorry. I didn't know."

"And that's why I'm telling you." He removed his hand from her arm, slowly, as if just realizing he'd had ahold of her. As if he didn't want to let go.

Something crazy was happening. It felt as if she was in a vortex, spinning ever so slowly, and he was in the middle of it with her. Looking into his eyes, she couldn't catch her breath. He felt it, too. He had to. The intensity of his gaze as he searched her face made it clear. She had to swim her way to the surface and break free.

"I need to go," she said. And then she glanced beyond him. "Allie!"

She pushed past him and ran to her daughter, catching her just as she fell. She should have been paying attention. She should have seen the distress in her daughter's eyes. With trembling hands Rebecca eased Allie onto her side as the seizure shook her small body.

Isaac knelt next to her. "Jack is calling Carson," he whispered.

"I don't know why this is happening." She shook her head. "That isn't true, I do know. It's the move. She had to leave her home, her school, her friends…"

"Don't blame yourself. You made the move because you thought in the long run it would be the best thing for her."

"Right. I thought my parents would…"

"What?"

She shook her head. "Nothing."

Jack appeared, his eyes full of concern as he studied her now-silent daughter.

"Carson said to bring her to his office so he can do a thorough examination."

Rebecca nodded and started to reach for her Allie. Isaac gently pushed her aside and lifted her daughter with care, holding her close. The tender look in his eyes almost undid Rebecca's composure. It wasn't fair that her child had to deal with this pain, with this illness.

As much as Rebecca knew it wasn't her fault, her father's words of accusation still taunted her, telling her that Allie suffered for her mother's sins.

"She's going to be okay," Isaac assured her as they headed for the door.

She nodded, unable to speak for fear tears would begin to fall and never stop. She'd been alone for so long. Her aunt had been ill for several years before her death. And afterward it had been easier to make it just her and Allie against the world.

After only a day in Hope, she was beginning to see how wrong she'd been. They did need people in their lives. They needed more than the safety net of knowing her parents were nearby.

She didn't need Isaac West, she just needed people. Maybe that would be her reason for staying in Hope. She and Allie would no longer be alone. They would have a community that surrounded them and cared for them.

But for some reason, that thought made her feel all the more lonely.

Chapter Five

Monday morning, a full week after her arrival in Hope, Rebecca sat in a chair in the center of what would soon be her salon. She'd dropped Allie off at school, made a stop at the feed store, where she'd found a good selection of interior paints, and then she'd called her parents.

Or tried to. Her mother had answered, sounding somewhat relieved to hear from her, and then she'd abruptly ended the call. Not before Rebecca had heard her father ask who was on the phone.

A wrong number, her mother had said as she hung up.

For years she'd been trying to convince herself it didn't hurt. But it did. And it never got easier.

She picked up the paint for her color scheme in the salon. A pale shell beige that would be warm and inviting with the wood floors and the brick back wall, and splashes of color to brighten it all.

The front door opened and she managed to stifle a groan. Isaac entered, removing his hat as he walked through the room. His gaze landed on the paint cans, brushes, rollers and pans. He grinned a little, spun on his heel and headed for the door he'd just come through.

She didn't know what to say. "Leaving so soon?"

He stopped, but didn't make a move to return. She couldn't help but smile.

"When I see a paintbrush I break out in hives. I'd rather crawl through a pigpen."

"That's a little extreme," she countered.

He settled his hat back on his head and looked at her, shooting her that trademark grin of his. He seemed to use it to charm, and to fool, people into thinking he was just fine. As he stood there watching her, he reached for a toothpick in his shirt pocket. Cinnamon. They were always cinnamon. The scent was strong as he pulled it from the package.

After only a week she already felt as if she knew him better than people she'd known for years. Of course, she'd felt she'd known Ryan Conners, the man she dated for six months. She'd even allowed him to meet Allie. After months of dating, she'd felt comfortable letting him into that part of her life.

She'd never guessed that the whole time they were dating he was busy planning his wedding to someone else. Obviously, she didn't read people as well as she thought she did.

"I won't ask you to paint." She pried a can open and stirred, ignoring the voice in her head that told her to tread softly with this man.

"I won't offer." He returned to her side, grabbing a folding chair to sit down in. "I did come here for a reason."

"Okay." She glanced up, meeting his warm gray eyes. He didn't smile, but his expression eased the tension that had been building in her since the failed phone call to her mother.

"We have a dog. Her name is Jersey, because I kind of think she has the eyes of a big old Jersey cow."

"I don't need a dog. I don't even know where I'm going to live."

"I assumed you were staying at the ranch."

"It's a ranch for wounded veterans. I'm not a veteran and I don't want to take space from those who might need it."

He sat there for a minute, his long, jean-clad legs stretched out in front of him, the toothpick sticking out of his teeth. After a minute he shifted it to the corner of his mouth and took the stir stick from her hand.

"I think you've been through some battles and you qualify as a wounded warrior."

"Don't give me that kind of credit. There's a huge difference between being a single mother and being willing to go to war."

"I joined the army because Jack told me I couldn't."

"But you went. I think you gave up a lot for your country." She stood, glancing around the room and noting the massive amount of work that needed to be done.

Plumbers had been there earlier that morning, discussing the best way to bring water to the areas where the sinks and pedicure stations would be, and the areas in the back that would later serve as a spa.

She'd found the chairs she wanted for her stylists. They were expensive, but she'd saved enough money to cover getting the salon up and running, as well as living expenses for several months.

"Let me help you paint," Isaac said.

"You said it gives you hives."

He pushed his hat back an inch and gave her a steady, dimpled look. "Yeah, well, I can take something for the hives. But I don't want to feel guilty, leaving a woman to do all of this painting alone. And we still have to discuss the dog."

"Jersey…" She repeated the name. "And why do you think we need a pet?"

"I didn't say she was a pet."

Now he seemed to be talking in riddles and Rebecca didn't have a clue what he meant. "Okay, so Jersey's not a pet?"

"She's a service animal."

"I don't understand."

He slipped an apron over his head to protect his shirt, grabbed a roller and glanced around the salon. She bit back a grin when he faced her, a cowboy in jeans, a button-up shirt, cowboy hat and flowery apron.

"Where do we start painting?"

"This wall where my sinks will be located." She pointed with a paintbrush.

"Gotcha." He stumbled a bit and she reached to help him, but then drew her hand back.

"Don't worry, I won't fall. I might wobble from time to time but it's a lot better than it was a few years ago. And that's an answer to prayer."

"Is it?" She immediately regretted the question. It sounded curious and skeptical. She didn't want to discuss faith. Not with this cowboy who wore a silver cross on a chain around his neck.

"Doubting Thomas," he said. "Yes, I believe in answered prayers. No, I'm not one hundred percent healthy, but I'm still here after a pretty serious head injury. I have headaches, an occasional struggle with balance and I can't hear out of my left ear. But I'm healthy and I'm alive."

She watched as he adjusted his expression. Yes, he was alive. And she knew it wasn't as easy as he wanted everyone to believe.

"About the dog," she said, changing the subject.

One dark brow arched. He knew what she was doing. She didn't care.

"Jersey is a sweetheart of a girl. She's been trained for soldiers with PTSD. I think she could help Allie."

"The soldiers are the ones who should have her. They need her. She can't stop my daughter from having a seizure."

"No, but she could do other things for Allie. If she happened to be alone, a dog could get help, retrieve medication or even comfort her and help her up afterward."

Rebecca knew all that. She had also read that after spending time with its owner, a service dog could sometimes predict the advent of a seizure.

"I can't afford an animal like that," she told him.

"Jersey isn't for sale."

"Then why tell me about her?"

"I talked to Jack and we both think that Jersey would make an excellent dog for Allie. We want to give you a dog that might make a difference in your daughter's life."

"Why?" The word came out strangled, frightened. She shook off the tidal wave of emotion that threatened to swamp her as his offer became clear.

People took from her. Other than Aunt Evelyn, no one ever gave to her. No one supported her or offered a shoulder to lean on.

"Because we can," Isaac replied quietly, gazing at her with eyes that saw too much. He reached for a roll of paper towels, tore a section off and handed it to her.

She swiped at tears, telling herself she shouldn't cry. She couldn't lose her composure. But more tears continued to fall even as she squeezed her eyes shut to stop the flow. Suddenly she felt strong arms around her and her head was tucked against a shoulder.

"You're just about the most stubborn woman I've ever met. You even fight tears."

She sniffled and laughed a little at the reprimand.

The front door opened. She quickly backed out of his embrace and turned to tell the person entering that the salon wasn't open yet. But the words didn't make it out. She stood watching as the woman who'd come in glanced around and then made eye contact.

"Rebecca," she said softly. Her brown hair had grayed and soft lines had etched the passage of time into her face.

Rebecca took a step back and shook her head. "Mother, what are you doing here?"

Isaac headed for the door. Rebecca moved quickly to his right side. "Stay."

He shook his head.

"It won't take long." She was trembling inside and hoped neither of them noticed. Her attention again moved to her mother. "Why are you here?"

Her mom closed the distance between them. "I wanted to see you. I'd like to meet my granddaughter."

"Her name is Allie and she's nine. Nine years old. It's been ten years since you sent me away."

"We didn't know what else to do." Her mother's voice broke as she made the excuse.

They were her parents. At eighteen, Rebecca had made a mistake and been sent away. They had told her that in time she would understand. But time had passed, she was a mother now and she understood even less. She couldn't imagine a transgression that would make her send Allie away.

"You could have loved me," she said. Her heart shattered a little at the knowledge that they hadn't loved her enough. They'd tried to wrap their rejection in love, telling her that their concern for her forced them to do this. For her own good.

"We did. We do love you."

"It doesn't feel like love."

Her mother's gaze dropped to the floor. "Why are you here?"

Rebecca nearly laughed. That was a good question. Why *was* she here?

"I'm not really sure. Maybe because I wanted to be close to home, close to you all. But I'm not ready to bring you into my daughter's life yet. I won't allow you to hurt her."

Alice Barnes's face crumpled. "I'm so sorry, Rebecca. Truly sorry. I hope in time you'll forgive me. And believe me when I tell you I have regretted every day of the past ten years."

"So have I."

Her mother sighed. "I also want to warn you to be careful. Don't let Greg back into your life."

Rebecca didn't know if she should laugh or cry. It hurt to think her mother thought so poorly of her. But then, Alice Barnes didn't really know her daughter.

"I have no intention of allowing him in my life or near my daughter. I was eighteen, Mother. I was a child who made a horrible mistake. I regret it. I wish there was forgiveness, the same mercy that my father preaches from his pulpit each week. But I want you to understand, my daughter is beautiful. I can't imagine my life without her."

Alice cried. "I hope you never have to experience life without her. I'll leave, but I hope in time we can see each other and that one day you'll allow me to know Allie."

Silent but still the gentleman, Isaac walked her mother to the door and opened it for her. After she left,

Rebecca sat in one of the folding chairs before her legs decided to give out.

Isaac faced her, his expression grim. She should have let him leave. He shouldn't have been forced to witness a family reunion that held only pain and anger.

She'd been weak, needing a friend to support her during that first encounter. She hadn't realized how devastating it would be to see her mother after so much time had passed.

Isaac pulled the other chair up and sat next to her. Slowly, he reached over, taking her hand in his.

Isaac didn't know what to say to the woman sitting next to him, devastated but still wearing that stoic facade of hers. He wanted to tell her she needed to scream. She needed to cry. She needed to do something other than sit there holding on to the pain.

The part of him that didn't want to be involved told him to leave her alone to lick her wounds. She didn't want or need him there. And he didn't want to be so involved in anyone's life.

But then her tears started to fall and he couldn't leave her. He had the strangest urge to take all her pain and make it his, so she wouldn't have to hurt this way.

He stood, though she didn't seem to notice. Removing the flowery apron he'd been wearing, he stepped behind her and wrapped her in a hug, leaning over her, sheltering her. He kissed the top of her head and told her she needed to cry.

Her cheek rested on his arm and her tears flowed, dampening his skin. She sobbed, heaving as the emotions rolled through her body.

"I don't like to cry," she sobbed.

"I know. Men and tears, the enemies."

She laughed a little and more tears fell. "I didn't expect it to hurt this much."

"I understand." He remembered watching his mom drive away when he was a little boy. He'd been fending for himself for as long as he could remember, but still, she'd been his mom.

"I've been telling myself for years that their rejection didn't matter. After all, I have the best thing in the world. I have Allie. She's beautiful, funny, smart. She's everything."

"I agree. And I'm not even much of a kid person."

She glanced up with tear-filled eyes. "You keep telling yourself that and someday you might believe it."

"Where is her dad?" he asked.

"Long story short, I went through a rebellious period at eighteen and he managed to convince me that we were in love. That love resulted in me unlocking the church for him to steal money for us to run away together. We were going to California to have Allie. My parents stopped us. They sent him away and shipped me off to my aunt Evelyn. Later he was arrested for armed robbery of a convenience store and went to prison."

"Not a nice guy." Isaac stated the obvious.

His arms were still around her and her hands had moved to hold them close. He should disengage. She would regret this later, telling him secrets, letting him hold her. He'd regret it, too, because it exposed something inside him that he hadn't expected to feel.

He wanted to hold her a little longer.

He wanted to tell her she was worth more. He wanted to tell her that what her father said or did wasn't important. *She* was important. Her child was worth everything.

Not his problem, he told himself. He shouldn't be involved. He was the last person anyone needed to count on.

He remembered all too well, in those first years, counting on Jack. He remembered being a kid and listening to Jack as the nightmares and the flashbacks had him in their grip.

Isaac would never put a woman or child through that torment.

He unwound his arms from her shoulders and she let him go, her hands sliding slowly from his biceps as he disengaged.

She looked up at him through teary eyes. Her lids were puffy and her hair framed her face, sticking to her cheeks. He pushed the tear-dampened strands from her face, tucking them behind her ear.

At that moment she needed reassurance. She needed a friend who would say and do the right thing. And he was a sorry excuse for a friend because he wanted to hold her again. Wanted to brush his lips across hers and inhale the sweet scent of roses and springtime.

Taking in a breath, he managed to get hold of himself. He squatted in front of her at eye level. Her gaze locked with his.

"I'm not an expert on all things spiritual."

She groaned, but he held up a hand and continued, "It's easy to walk away from God and church when the pain comes from inside those walls, inflicted by the very people who should show us love and compassion. Mercy. The world is filled with casualties, walking wounded, the people like you who want nothing to do with God, with church, because someone hurt them. I'm just asking you to seek God. Let Him touch your life and take some of this pain."

Her eyes fluttered closed as she nodded. He nearly ran his hand through her honey-blond hair, but he stopped himself in time.

"I'm not sure if I can," she answered honestly. "I've been angry for so long."

"I get that," he told her as he straightened. "I've been there."

"Have you?" She paused. "Care to share?"

"I'd rather not. At least not right now."

Her head cocked to the side. "That isn't fair, is it? You know my stories. But I don't know yours."

"I don't have stories. Not really."

"Really?" she asked. "I find that hard to believe. Your mother left you with Jack when you were a little boy, not much older than Allie is now."

"Yeah, but I was used to fending for myself."

"You were a child," she pressed.

"Never," he said, with a teasing smile.

She studied him for a moment, appearing ready to argue. Instead of asking more questions, she glanced around the salon. "I'm done crying. I have a business to open. And I plan to have it ready to go in two weeks."

"That's an ambitious goal."

"I know." Her blue eyes lit up with mirth. "But with your help it should be doable."

With his help. That put him front and center in her life.

He took the paintbrush and allowed her to put him to work. The job gave him something to focus on. Something other than her springtime scent and the memory of the tears that had spilled from her eyes.

Chapter Six

She had dark hair, dark eyes, a sad smile. She always appeared to be hungry. So they fed her. They called her Sally, because her name was foreign to their American tongues, and they gave her toys. Isaac ordered her a doll and when it arrived he wrapped it in purple paper, the color she seemed to like the most.

For several days she didn't come around. None of them had time to go hunting for a child who didn't seem to belong to anyone. And then they saw her. She slipped down the street, peering back at them as if she couldn't escape fast enough.

They heard the gunfire. They yelled at her to stop. She kept running, running. And then the world exploded around them. The last time he saw her, she was falling. Screaming. He hadn't been able to help.

Isaac sat up in a cold sweat, his heart racing. He sat for a moment, listening. No one came running. The house was silent. Joe would have earplugs in. The others were probably lost in their own nightmares. He got up and walked to the window. The gray light of early morning was creeping across the eastern horizon.

After a few minutes he shrugged into a jacket, pulled on his boots and headed downstairs. He needed work to get his mind off the nightmare. And coffee. Thanks to a timer, the coffee maker had started and the pot was half-filled. He poured a cup and headed out the back door.

There were lights on in the main house. Jack lived there alone, but Maria, the housekeeper and cook, showed up early every morning. She spoiled Jack. Isaac figured she was half in love with the old coot, the way she looked out for him. Jack seemed oblivious. Someone ought to point it out to him before he broke her heart. Or wasted the years he had left, alone and with a good woman right under his nose.

Not that Isaac was bent on matchmaking. He wouldn't want anyone trying to arrange his life that way. Some people were better left alone with their nightmares.

The cup of coffee steamed in the cool morning air. Christmas was less than four weeks away and even if it wasn't beginning to look a lot like Christmas, it sure felt like it. They needed trees.

He sipped his coffee and contemplated the holidays with a child at the ranch. Children. Carson and Kylie's two, Maggie and Andy, would be there. Isaac kind of enjoyed the uncle gig. He spoiled them and sent them home. Maybe Colt and Daisy would even stop by. Nah, that would never happen. His half siblings were a pretty angry bunch.

They would include Allie if she and her mother were still at the ranch.

"What's got you looking so serious?"

The question startled him and he nearly spilled his coffee. He glanced back at the woman coming down the sidewalk in her wheelchair.

"Good morning, Evie. What are you up to?"

"You didn't answer my question," she said, refraining from reminding him that she didn't like to be called Evie.

He grinned, ignoring the fire in her eyes.

"I'm heading to the barn. I've got a mare that looks like she might foal in the next few days. I'm also going to work with my mare."

Eve rolled to a stop, her hands resting on the wheels of her chair. "You're not good at this."

"At what?"

"At pretending you're not distracted. And only one thing—or two—have changed around here in the past week."

"You're barking up the wrong tree." Speaking of barking, he needed to talk to Kylie about the dog, Jersey. He should have done that before he offered the animal to Allie.

"Okay, we can play the game your way. You're not interested. You still have the rule about no long-term relationships."

"You're still meddling in my business and you need to concern yourself with your own life. How are the folks?"

"That's a low blow."

He sighed and pushed his hat back. "I know. I'm sorry."

Her relationship with her parents was her own business. And then there was the fiancé she'd broken up with.

"Stop. I don't want to discuss my life or yours." She pushed her chair forward again. "Oh, one thing. Have you talked to your aunt Lola lately?"

"Not this week." Guilt slammed him hard. He'd never gone a week without checking on his mother's aunt Lola. The elderly woman had done her best to keep track of him when he was young.

"Joe said he saw her yesterday. She was sitting down by the lake with a fishing pole and no bait. He gave her a ride back to her apartment."

Isaac took off his hat and ran a hand through his short hair. "I'll get by there this afternoon."

She stopped following him. "Isaac?"

He glanced back. "Yeah?"

"We women don't always plan on falling in love. Sometimes we think we're immune, kind of like you. But when a nice guy comes along, it just happens."

"You love me?" he teased.

"Not me. Ever. You're like…a cat."

"That's the best you've got?"

She shrugged. "I don't like cats but I tolerate them. They serve a purpose."

"I'm not going to get enmeshed and I'm not breaking any hearts."

"There's a child involved," she warned.

"I know that and I appreciate the advice." Even if it was unnecessary. "And thanks for the update on Lola."

She turned back to the garage apartment and he headed for the stable that had taken the place of the barn that had been there when he was a kid. It had been a great barn. Wood siding, metal roof and a hayloft. The stable looked like every other big, expensive building of its kind. Metal siding, indoor arena, a dozen stalls, office, feed and tack rooms.

He pushed open the double doors at the front and entered. For a moment he stood in the softly lit interior, the scents of hay, horses and cedar all combining to make one of his favorite smells in the world. Hooves stomped as the animals moved in their stalls. A few heads came over stall doors to whinny a greeting. It didn't matter that he was early; they were ready for breakfast. So was he. Before the horses got fed he was going to grab another cup of coffee and a protein bar from the office.

On the way past Mouse's stall, he heard the mare squeal at him. Isaac stopped to peek in. Still no foal, but she wasn't happy with the labor process. And she appeared to be further on than he would have expected. He opened the stall door and stepped inside. She pawed at the ground and shied away, giving a warning swish of her tail.

"Easy, Mouse. You know me." He remained close to her side, running a hand down her gray neck. "There you go. Easy, girl."

She gave his sleeve a light nip.

"I'm going to get coffee and I'll be back." He gave her another pat on the neck. "Can I get you anything?"

"She can't really talk, can she?" a small voice asked from the other side of the door.

He saw the child most likely to sneak away from her mother standing there. "Do you ever warn a guy before you sneak up on him?"

She giggled. "Did I scare you again?"

"Not at all. Does your mother know you're out here?"

She shook her head.

"You're going to get us both in trouble, Allie." He reached for her hand. "Come on, let's get you back to the house. Don't you have school today?"

"Dr. Carson said I can't go today. He thinks I need to rest. Is he your brother?"

"Half brother." Did a girl her age understand? "Yes, he's my brother."

He led her out of the barn and toward the women's apartments.

"My mom isn't in there."

He stopped walking. "Where is she?"

"Jack's house. She's fixing breakfast because Maria is sick. She was in the pantry and I saw you going to the stable."

"Okay, kid, listen. We have to establish some rules."

She looked crestfallen so he gave her hand a reassuring squeeze. "Nothing serious, just rules to keep you safe. First, you don't go anywhere without telling your mom or another responsible adult."

"Like you?" she asked.

"No. I said a responsible adult. Everyone will tell you I'm the farthest thing from responsible."

"You look responsible to me." She glanced up at him, studying his face.

"Looks can be deceiving." He led her toward the house. "Let's get back to the list of rules."

The back door of Jack's house swung open with a bang. He looked up as Rebecca came out, saw them and went from relieved to angry.

"Uh-oh," Allie whispered.

"Yeah, uh-oh. This is why we have rule number one. Rule number two, apologize. Rule number three, you don't go in the stable or pastures without permission and without an adult."

"That's a lot of rules."

"Yeah, start with number two."

Rebecca approached, her gaze landing on her daughter and then on him.

He nudged Allie.

"I'm sorry, Mom," she said in a small voice. "I saw Isaac walking to the barn and wanted to go. But he said to apologize and follow rule number one—no going anywhere without telling you or a responsible adult. And he isn't responsible."

Her angry demeanor cracked a bit and a hint of amusement flickered in her eyes. "You're supposed to be inside resting."

"I know, but Isaac went to the barn and I—"

"Rule number four, no arguing." Rebecca held out a hand for her daughter to take. "Tell Isaac you'll see him later."

"You'll have to bring her out soon. We're about to have a new foal."

"I can't miss a new foal!" Allie spoke quickly. "Can we watch?"

"The mare actually doesn't like an audience. She waits for us to walk away." From the stable he heard a loud, pained whinny. "And then she has the baby."

Allie shot a worried look in the direction of the barn. "Is she okay?"

"Yes, she's okay. I'm going back out there, and when your mom is ready, she can bring you on out to check on things."

"We'll eat breakfast with Jack and then we'll be out to see how things are going," Rebecca responded, still holding tight to Allie's hand. She probably thought if she loosened her grip, the little girl would run for the stable.

He watched as the two of them headed for the house, a matched set, mother and daughter. As he stood there in the yard, the grass crunchy beneath his boots as he shifted his weight, Allie glanced back at him.

Brown eyes, a hazy morning, and then an explosion and she disappeared into the thick smoke. It was the last thing he remembered before waking up in an army hospital in Germany.

He scrubbed his hands down his face and reminded himself that this wasn't Afghanistan. The little girl heading for the house wasn't that Afghan child. He breathed deeply, taking an inventory of his surroundings, listening for the familiar sounds of Mercy Ranch and not the streets of a war-torn land.

And he prayed. Because he didn't want to get lost in the memories.

"You okay?"

He shook himself free from his thoughts and realized Jack was standing in front of him. Jack, who knew the way a moment could drag a guy into a flashback. A memory that felt so real he thought he was still living that day. Over and over again.

He'd stopped it this time. He'd managed to hold on to reality.

Behind Jack stood Rebecca and Allie. The little girl appeared to be oblivious to his turmoil. Rebecca studied him intently, seeing far too much.

"I'm good. Just got lost in thought."

"You've been standing there for several minutes," Jack warned, his voice low.

"Meditating," he said. "It's a beautiful morning. I can feel Christmas in the air."

He winked at Allie. She didn't appear to buy his excuse any more than Jack or her mother did. His gaze collided with Rebecca's. Honey-blond hair framed her face and her brown eyes appeared concerned. For him.

From the stables a horse whinnied. He said something about checking on Mouse. And of course they all tagged along.

Rebecca followed Jack and Isaac, not listening to their conversation as they approached the barn, but hearing enough to understand. Isaac West had nightmares. Or possibly flashbacks.

She'd seen him out the window as Allie had been pleading her case for escaping, and then asking to please go see the new foal. Jack had joined them, taking Allie's side, and then he'd seen Isaac standing in the yard. It had been obvious, even from a distance, that something had happened.

Jack had muttered under his breath and headed out the door. Rebecca had followed, drawn because she couldn't not care. As they got closer, she'd seen the panic on Isaac's face. She'd seen the lost expression as he'd come back to himself.

Whatever had happened, he was himself again. Or a good imitation. He opened the door, revealing the mare. She paced around the stall, then stopped to paw the ground. After a few minutes she took another turn, then paused again. This time she kicked at her belly and then heaved and settled to the floor. Her body tensed with the force of her contraction and she shuddered, whinnying softly at the man who remained inside her domain.

Jack stood just outside the stall door, Allie close to his side, her mouth open in awe.

The mare stood again, circled the enclosure, kicking at her belly, stretching as another contraction hit. When she moved to the corner of the stall and tried to lower herself once more, Isaac took hold of her halter and drew her forward several feet.

"Away from the wall, Mousy girl." He soothed her as she eased to the ground. "It won't be long, Allie."

Allie, wide-eyed, nodded. Rebecca stepped close to her daughter. "If this is too much, we can come back later."

"Mom," she said with meaning. "I want to see this. It might be gross, but it's a baby horse."

"Almost a baby horse," Jack said, as he pulled a stool close and took a seat. "And it will be gross. But beautiful."

His gray eyes misted over with unshed tears. "Best part of ranching is new life. Physically and spiritually."

"Getting sentimental on me, Jack?" Isaac asked as he stood back, giving the mare some room.

"I'm old. I'm allowed." Jack nodded, indicating they should watch the foaling process.

Mousy, as Isaac had called her, continued to push. It took time but eventually half the foal emerged. They waited.

"Should you help?" Allie asked.

Isaac shook his head, but he didn't take his eyes off the mare and foal. "No, we wait. It's resting. So is its mama. Being born takes a lot of work. If either of them is in distress, we'll give them some help. Right now, even though it's taking a while, this is all normal."

Rebecca pointed, now as excited as Allie. The foal's body slid to the straw. Isaac still waited.

"It's resting and getting what it needs from the mama."

Finally, Isaac knelt next to the foal and wiped its nostrils, eyes, ears.

"Sometimes a baby can't quite get free. That's why we're here. Not that Mousy wouldn't have seen to it. But we don't want to take any chances. Allie, I think you should name—" Isaac took a closer look "—name her."

Allie watched with all the wonder in the world reflected in her eyes.

Jack put a hand on her shoulder. "Kind of makes a person a little teary, doesn't it. And when I see this at Christmas, I think of that little baby born in a lowly barn, surrounded by animals and shepherds."

"Christmas," Allie whispered. "Her name should be Christmas."

"Maybe that's too much name for such a small animal," Rebecca offered.

The tiny foal, a replica of her mouse-gray mother, was kicking to get up. She did kind of look like Christmas with her spunky little face, bright eyes and brushy black tail.

"I think that's a perfect name for this little filly," Jack said with a firm nod. "She's a dandy, Isaac. You were right about that stallion and Mouse. They're going to make some mighty fine offspring. Little Christmas will be a winner. Now, if you all don't mind, I'm going to head to the house. Isaac, when you get a moment, introduce the girls to Jersey."

"I'll take them to the kennel as soon as this little girl is eating." Isaac stepped back from the foal and mare, giving Jack a quick smile.

Jack left, moving somewhat slower than he had been earlier. Rebecca watched him make his way down the aisle of the stable and out into the sunlight. She turned her attention back to Allie, who stood just inside the stall, watching the foal named Christmas as she did her best to stand on wobbly legs.

Isaac looked more cornered than awestruck at that moment.

"You don't have to show us the dog," Rebecca murmured, giving him a way out.

He eased slowly from the stall, closing the door behind them, allowing mare and foal to have their moment. His hand rested on Allie's shoulder and the two of them eased back a step as the mare nudged her foal.

It was a moment. A moment when the three of them stood there at the stall door in the early morning quiet. Allie climbed on Jack's stool to get a better view over the top of the door, and as they watched, the foal found its mother and nestled against her.

"Aww," Allie whispered.

"This is what makes life on the ranch pretty close to perfect," Isaac said. Then his arm settled around Rebecca's shoulders, drawing her close.

She started to pull away, but something in how he tugged her to his side told her that this wasn't just about the foal, a perfect morning or even him being the flirty cowboy she'd first pegged him to be.

The embrace felt more like a man seeking the comfort of the person standing next to him. She'd had more than a few of those instances herself, when she'd just needed someone to hold her.

As a woman, she could admit to those moments. She'd had one yesterday, when he'd held her after her mom left the shop. His arm tightened around her, saying more than words. Her heart got tangled up, wondering what it meant about her, that she wanted to be the person he leaned on in that moment of weakness.

Chapter Seven

Isaac watched for a while as the foal nursed, then he slipped away to clean up, leaving Rebecca and her daughter with the horses. It mattered that she'd been standing there with him. He didn't know why, it just did. Deep down it felt as if she'd taken a little of his pain, his burden, away.

He didn't want her to do that, but man, it had felt good, holding her. He knew she couldn't make him whole. He knew that God had already done that, and there were still things he'd have to work through, deal with, live with. But after the morning he'd had, Rebecca had been a balm for his troubled soul.

Not that he was going all poetic or romantic. She'd been the right person at the right time, that was all.

He left the office, buttoning up his clean shirt as he went. Rebecca and Allie were gone. And just like that, he felt empty again.

"Shouldn't you be smiling?" Joe walked through the stable, his own shirt buttoned crooked, his grin a little too happy.

"Why should I smile?"

"New filly?"

"Oh, Christmas," he responded.

Joe looked confused. "I don't know what you're talking about, but I was talking about Mouse's new foal."

"Her name is Christmas." Isaac moved forward, unbuttoning the flannel shirt Joe had thrown over a T-shirt. Two years ago, when Joe had first showed up at Mercy Ranch, Isaac would have left the buttons.

Something happened to a bunch of men when they started being each other's hands, eyes, ears. They got used to depending on one other. Even when it felt uncomfortable.

"Thanks, Mom." Joe grinned again as Isaac buttoned his shirt up right. "I'll never tell anyone that you know how to be a decent human being. No one would believe it anyway."

"You're killing me with kindness this morning."

"Bad night?"

"No, why?"

"I've known you a few years and can tell when you've had nightmares. Plus you threw something at my wall during the night, shook my whole room."

"Sorry." Isaac cracked his knuckles because some kind of manly gesture was needed.

"So the foal's name is Christmas. Going to tell me why?"

"Allie named her."

Joe's eyes widened.

"I have to go." Isaac grabbed his jacket off a peg. "Do you mind hooking a round bale and hauling it to the steers?"

"Nope, I can do it. I sent a few guys to town to the bait factory. You know I saw Lola?"

"Yeah. I'll check on her soon. I'm introducing Allie to Jersey."

"Jersey?"

He wished he hadn't said anything. The more he said, the deeper he dug the hole. It didn't take a guy long to recognize the looks, to know what people were thinking. Allie had named the horse. Jack had recommended the dog. Joe, and probably others, were thinking something was going on between him and Rebecca. She was a nice woman. Her daughter was pretty terrific. The last thing he needed in his life was a woman. A child definitely not.

"Jack and I discussed it. The kid needs a dog."

"Gotcha," Joe said. "And Allie and her mom are with Kylie. Looks like they're hauling decorations out of the shed. It's that time of year."

"Thanks." Isaac headed for the double doors at the front of the building. "Hey, I'm going to try to work Penny and Buster."

"You do that. I'm not getting on one of your cutting horses."

Isaac stopped at the doors. "You're a better rider than you give yourself credit for. Considering you're a city boy."

Joe laughed at that. "Yeah, well, I'm not denying it."

"Catch you later." Isaac headed in the direction of the storage shed. He could see Allie and Rebecca with Kylie. Allie had silver garland wrapped around her like a shawl. Kylie handed her a small container of decorations.

In unison the three glanced his way, Allie waving with her free hand.

"Are we bringing in the trees today?" he asked.

Kylie pulled a tub out of the shed and stacked it on one already in a small wagon. "Yes, we are. And I can't wait. It's the first of December and with these mild temperatures it just doesn't feel like Christmas. We need to get these decorations up."

"How does Christmas feel?" he teased.

She frowned at him. "It feels like tinsel, chocolate candy, cinnamon candles, soup." She pulled something from a container. "And mistletoe."

She held up a sprig of fake mistletoe over Rebecca's head. Rebecca started to back away, but Allie lassoed her with the garland.

"You have to kiss her," Allie said. "It's bad luck if you don't."

"That isn't a thing," Isaac told her.

She nodded, as if she truly believed it.

"I don't believe in luck," he informed her. "I believe in faith. Faith always trumps luck."

"If you don't kiss her she'll think you don't like her," Allie teased.

Isaac stared at the woman in question. Her cheeks were pink now and the breeze blew strands of blond hair that had come loose from her ponytail. Kylie had tossed the mistletoe back in the container, but it didn't seem to matter. Allie unwound the garland and returned to perusing the tub that held the nativity set.

"I wouldn't want you to think I don't like you," Isaac said, winking at her. Then he kissed her. It was meant to be carefree, but the moment his lips touched hers, he realized his mistake.

She tasted sweet, like strawberry jam. She tasted like a woman who should have forever with a man who would never let her down, never make her fear. He couldn't make that promise to any woman.

"Hey, the mistletoe is gone," Kylie teased, but a warning edged into her tone.

Isaac backed away. Rebecca's gaze crashed against his, asking questions. He didn't have answers.

He wasn't about to apologize. He cleared his throat. "We should go meet Jersey." He glanced away, needing a moment.

"We don't have to. If y-you have something else you need to do," Rebecca stammered. "I mean, I have to go to the shop and finish painting. And some of the equipment and supplies I ordered should be delivered today and tomorrow."

"It will only take a minute to meet the dog. We can take her to town with us, so she and Allie can see how they like each other."

Allie rolled her eyes. "I always get along with dogs."

He gave her a steady look. She was a smart kid and he wasn't going to talk down to her or pretend she wouldn't understand.

"I bet you do, but it's different with a dog like Jersey. You'll be more than friends. She'll go everywhere with you. She'll be more than a pet. She'll be a lot like your mom. She'll look out for you."

"I see. So we have to bond?"

"Yeah, you have to bond. And if you don't bond with her, we won't waste time. We'll look at other dogs."

"Let's go, then." Allie glanced back at her mom. "Are you okay?"

"Yes, of course. I'm fine. Let's go meet Jersey."

"I can help you get that in the house," Isaac offered, as Kylie continued to fill the wagon.

She pulled a cobweb from her hair and blew a strand

of hair off her face. "I'm good. Carson will be here in a few hours and he'll help me get it inside. If you're around at lunchtime, you can help, too."

"I'll be around."

As they headed for the kennel Allie slipped between him and Rebecca. She skipped along next to them. And then she was holding his hand and her mother's, uniting them.

"We're bonding," she said. "Like I'll do with the dog. That's how you learn if you'll be a good team."

"Allie, you have to stop." Rebecca turned a dark pink. If Allie was being put up to this, it wasn't by her mother. He'd put everything he had on that being the truth.

"I'm sorry." Allie continued to hold his hand in her left, her mother's in her right. She skipped along between them, and she didn't look sorry.

"Is that Jersey?" she asked. The pale, almost white, yellow Lab barked.

"That's her." He released her hand and led her through the gate into the small cottage that housed kennels where the dogs slept. There was also a pantry where they kept dog food, leashes, collars and other supplies, and he headed that way.

When he returned Allie was on her knees outside the pen and Jersey was licking her fingers through the chain link. The little girl looked up, a wide grin splitting her face.

"I love this dog."

"I thought you might." He opened the gate and snapped a leash on the dog. "Let's take her for a walk."

A phone rang. Rebecca reached in her pocket and pulled hers out. She studied the number and then she sighed. "I have to take this."

"Mom," Allie said as she walked away.

He watched her go, a feeling of dread settling in his stomach. But she didn't need his interference. Not that he wasn't interfering. Of course he was. The dog was interfering. His help at her shop. All ways that he was getting involved in her business. He should know better. Nothing good could come from a relationship between the two of them. Even friendship with Rebecca and her daughter seemed too complicated.

Rebecca listened as her mother sobbed, apologizing, telling her she was in danger. She wanted this all to be a figment of her imagination, a bad dream, anything other than the truth.

"Mom, please tell me what's going on."

Her mother sobbed into the phone. "Your father got a call from a police officer. He wanted us to get a message to you—that Greg might be heading to Arizona. We had no reason to believe it wasn't a police officer, so your father explained that Aunt Evelyn had passed away and left you a little money and that you're living in Hope and starting a business, but that you would be safe because you're close to family."

"And it was Greg?" Rebecca already knew the answer to that question. Of course it was Greg. Now he knew where to find her. She held the phone and listened to her mother, but her gaze traveled to where Allie knelt with the dog, Jersey. Isaac watched Allie, but occasionally his attention switched to her.

"It'll be okay," she assured her mother.

"I hope so. Maybe you should come here."

Now? After all this time and the words said between them? "No, I can't."

She wouldn't.

"If you need us…" Her mother spoke quietly, as if she knew Rebecca would never turn to them for help.

Not that she didn't want her parents in her life. But she wanted them to give her unconditional love. She wanted them to love her daughter. It had been ten years, but the memory of being dragged to the front of the church on a Sunday morning, where her father had listed her sins to the congregation, was as fresh in her mind as it had been the day it happened.

"I have to go."

"You'll call if you need us?" Her mother repeated the earlier offer.

"Yes, of course."

Rebecca ended the call. She shoved her phone in her pocket and smiled when Allie waved and pointed to the dog. Rebecca nodded, still too shaken to approach her daughter. She needed a minute to breathe, to focus.

To pray that everything wouldn't fall apart. Pray. She had prayed on occasion. As angry as she'd been at her parents, at God, at the church, she still needed to know that someone cared. In a lonely world she needed to know that someone out there had some inkling she existed and needed help.

At the moment she needed all the help she could get. She felt like the worst kind of fraud and hypocrite, calling out to a God she'd turned away from.

"Are you okay?" Isaac stood close to her, his cowboy hat pulled down low, casting his features in shadowy appeal.

"I'm fine." No, that wasn't the truth. She'd never felt so alone, not even when her parents put her on the bus to Arizona to go live with Aunt Evelyn.

It had been a few years since she'd had anyone to

lean on, to talk to. The two men she'd dated hadn't ever wanted to hear about her day, her life, her child.

Now, she had Isaac. He wanted to know if she was okay. He truly seemed to care. His shoulder bumped hers, a reminder that he was standing next to her, waiting.

His concern filled up something inside her, something that had been hollow with yearning. She hadn't realized until this moment that she was lonely.

"You're not fine," he said after a few minutes. "I'm not much good at eavesdropping." He pointed to his left ear. "But I'm good at reading faces."

"You don't want to get involved in this," she warned him.

He laughed. "You're right, I don't. I'm very good at not getting involved. But I think someone needs to be, so here I am. Involved."

Allie approached with Jersey. Unlike many dogs Rebecca had known, Jersey didn't pull on the leash. When a barn cat ran across the yard, the dog's tail wagged but she remained close to Allie. And Allie obviously loved the Labrador.

"I think we bonded," Allie said, as she studied her mother's face. "That call was about my father, wasn't it? I mean, he isn't really my father if I don't know him and he's never been part of my life. But I think he's done something bad again."

"You don't have to worry," Rebecca assured her.

"Do you think I'll grow up to be like him?"

"Not at all. I think you'll grow up to be who you are. Smart, funny, caring. And all of those traits will grow as you grow."

Allie put an arm around the Labrador. "We don't have to leave here, do we?"

"Eventually, yes. Because we will have to find our own home. But we will be staying in Hope."

"I like it on the ranch," Allie informed her. "And I like Jersey."

"I know you do, but you can't keep her. She belongs to Mr. West and the people that live on the ranch."

"We'll discuss that," Isaac interjected. "Jersey has a problem. She isn't fond of the men on the ranch. And the women have Maximus."

"He sleeps in the apartment." Allie told him. "Can I walk Jersey over to Miss Kylie, so she can see that we've bonded?"

Rebecca glanced around, spotting Kylie back at the shed, loading up more Christmas decorations. She looked up at the sky, now devoid of sunshine. Clouds had rolled in, the light gray clouds of winter. It was too warm for snow, but the clouds had that look about them.

"You may go over and speak to her, but then come right back to me. It's getting cooler and it might rain."

Allie hugged her tightly. "Thank you. I love you."

"I love you, too."

The words released a few tears that she quickly brushed away before Allie could see. She watched her daughter dart away, the dog at her side, and she wished it could always be this way. She wished Allie could always be a child, always smiling and innocent.

Isaac moved a little closer to her side. He took her by the hand and she immediately felt stronger. Though she wanted to pull back, she needed that strength. He led her to a bench near the kennel.

"She's never met her father?" he asked, as they sat down.

Rebecca shook her head. "No. He's been in prison. I just want her to be a child, happy and safe."

"She might want to meet him someday," he offered.

"She might."

The thought was too much. Rebecca closed her eyes, wanting to block all thoughts of that inevitable time when Allie would meet her father.

The wind picked up, bringing a quick drop in temperature. A few raindrops fell from the wintery gray sky. Isaac took her hand in his and pulled her to her feet.

"It's about to start raining." He hurried her around the kennel and toward the house.

Even from a distance she could see Kylie herding Allie and the dog through the back door of Jack's house. The sky opened up and cold rain started to fall. Isaac switched directions. Rebecca tried to pull away from him, in the direction of the house, but his hand on hers held tight.

"We can get to the stable quicker than the house." He ran in that direction, pulling her along with him.

"But Allie…"

"Kylie won't let her out of her sight."

They rushed through the open doors of the stable, and once inside, Isaac pushed the doors closed. Rebecca hugged herself. She was soaked to the bone and freezing. Isaac didn't seem at all bothered by the sudden change in weather.

"Let's get you a warm jacket," he offered, as he led the way through the stable. "And some coffee."

"Both sound great."

He motioned her through the door of the office. As soon as they were inside, he rummaged in a closet, finding a lined sweatshirt that he tossed to her. As she pulled it on, he started a fresh pot of coffee.

Isaac picked up a towel and, after he'd dried his face and hair, handed it to her. "Need this?"

She shook her head. But that was silly. It was a towel and she needed it. She reached for it, but he didn't let go. Instead he used the towel to pull her close. Close enough that she smelled the clean scent of him. Soap, coffee, rain. Her senses filled with his scent, his presence.

Slowly, he reached for her, sliding his hand along her jaw. He tilted her head and touched his lips to hers.

It wasn't what she expected, that kiss. She hadn't expected to stand there as his mouth explored hers. She should have pulled away, but couldn't convince herself not to want this moment in his arms, feeling cherished.

As much as she tried to relegate herself to a box labeled Single Mom, his kiss made her feel like a woman. In his arms she was more. His kiss made her feel less alone.

His lips moved, hovering near her temple as he held her close. It was just a kiss. A kiss from a man who had been kind, tender, reserved, teasing.

The door opened. He stepped back, a smile hovering on his lips as he continued to stare at her. She turned away, brushing the towel over her face.

One of the men from the ranch, Joe, entered. He gave them both a curious look and then headed for the coffeepot without commenting.

As if he hadn't noticed.

No one ever had to know. But Rebecca would know. She would try to pretend it hadn't happened. She was sure Isaac would do the same. It was for the best, she told herself.

The last thing she needed as she started a new life for herself and Allie here in Oklahoma was more complications. With that in mind she escaped, braving the rain as she ran for the house.

Chapter Eight

Isaac unfolded a lawn chair next to the one his aunt Lola sat in. She glanced at him but didn't seem to know him. He didn't allow that to bother him. What difference would it make? He could get upset, hurt, frustrated, but in the end she would still be Aunt Lola and she would still have dementia.

After a few minutes she put down her fishing pole and gave him a long look, recognition finally dawning. "Did you get out of school early?"

He shook his head. It wouldn't do any good to tell her he'd been out of school for a long time. "No, it's Wednesday and I'm on my way to church. I didn't find you at your apartment earlier so I came here. I figured you'd be down here fishing."

In front of them, Grand Lake of the Cherokee sparkled. The winter sunset reflected across the clear but darkening waters. A short distance out a fish jumped, leaving ripples that caught the waning sunlight. And overhead a bird swooped, skimming low across the water.

Calm swept over him as he sat there with Aunt Lola. She had always been a little eccentric, living in her one-room home with no indoor plumbing. She'd worked at a factory and saved most of what she earned. He thought she had close to seven figures in her savings account. He kept that to himself. The last thing he needed were people coming out of the woodwork to steal from her.

"I didn't know you were looking for me," she said. She pulled the fishing pole back and cast it again, letting the hookless line float over the water and then slowly flutter down to the surface.

"No, I reckon you didn't. I was worried about you, though."

"More like you were worried about yourself. Is your mama out running again? That woman couldn't be faithful if the Good Lord himself asked."

He started to tell her his mother left town years ago. No one had seen or heard from her since she dropped him at Jack's. It had been close to twenty years now. He'd looked for her, checking the usual social media sites. Nothing ever came of it.

"I'm not worried about myself, Aunt Lola. I'm a grown man, remember?"

She reeled in the line and then gave him another long look.

"Well, I reckon you have grown up. You ever going to get married?"

"No, ma'am, I'm not. No woman needs to deal with all this." He gestured to himself.

"Oh, I think you'd make a fine husband. You're a little like your father but not so much that it would hurt."

Not so much that it would hurt. But he wouldn't take a chance. Jack had left scars, some visible and some deep down, hidden from view but still there. He stood, folding his lawn chair and giving a last longing look at the lake. He'd like to be out there fishing. It would be a good night for being on a boat. Cool but still and peaceful.

The sun was setting low on the western horizon. The temperature was dropping at a rapid rate.

"Let's go to church," he told his aunt. "They're serving spaghetti tonight. If we hurry they might have some left."

"I suppose I can go, since you're being so rude about it. I don't know why you get like that. And why would you want spaghetti when I've made you some of those ramen noodles you like so much?"

He helped her to her feet and planted a kiss on her cheek.

"Aunt Lola, we don't eat those noodles anymore. Remember, too much salt and they're bad for your blood pressure."

"Hmm, I suppose we don't. Well, let's go to church. You always were a good boy. I can't understand why Charlene left you the way she did."

He didn't want to talk about his mother and why she'd left him. But he'd survived and for that he was thankful. He led his aunt up the hill away from the lake. His truck was parked near the boat ramp. From where they stood he could see the shops on Lakeside Drive. He could see Rebecca's little car parked in front of her salon. He hadn't seen her since yesterday. Following the kiss she'd run off like a scalded cat, and shortly after she'd gone to town to work on her shop.

He might as well stop by and see if she wanted to go to church. He knew the answer, but he had a stubborn streak.

When he pulled up to the salon, she and Allie were just coming out. And Jersey. Rebecca locked the door, then spotted him in his truck. She shook her head, but she didn't walk away like he thought she might.

He rolled down his window, letting in the cool air of early December.

"I thought I'd invite you to church," he said. "They're going to start practicing for the Christmas program. I thought Allie might enjoy that. She can meet some of the kids."

Allie started to jump up and down, but then looked at her mother, and it brought her back down to earth, her smile evaporating as quickly as rain on a hot summer day.

Rebecca shot him a glare that clearly said she didn't want his interference. He grinned at that look, all fiery and sweet. Maybe that's what she'd been missing out on, someone interfering in her life. In a good way.

He'd had a constant flow of people interfering in his life, pushing him when he didn't want to be pushed, keeping him from getting too complacent, moving him forward when it would have been easy to crawl in a dark hole somewhere.

Rebecca looked down at her daughter and her expression softened. He saw her exhale and lift her eyes to meet his.

"Okay, fine."

"Do you need to follow us?" he asked Rebecca as she opened her car door.

"No, I've seen it. Brick church, down Second Street?"

"That's the one. Just go down Lakeside to the second road to the right."

"I'll meet you there."

"Oh, my," Aunt Lola teased. "What did you do to her?"

"I invited her to church," he said.

"Well, remember the Bible says not to be unequally yoked."

"I'm not yoking myself to anyone. I invited her to

church. That's all. Her little girl will enjoy being part of the Christmas program."

"I do like spaghetti. I hope Mattie made it. She's the best cook in the county. Not that Holly isn't a decent cook. But she's young and still has some things to learn. Although she does make me a mighty fine fried bologna sandwich."

He glanced at his aunt, puzzled. "She doesn't have fried bologna on the menu."

"No, she doesn't, but she does make it and brings it to me when I'm fishing."

He would have to thank Holly for that.

A few minutes later they were standing on the sidewalk in front of the church waiting for Rebecca and Allie to join them. Allie and Jersey led the way. The dog perked up when she saw Isaac, but she did him proud, not pulling on the harness. Her tail wagged but she remained next to her girl. And Allie grinned, proud of her new companion.

It did his battered heart good to see the little girl and the dog together. He knew Jersey couldn't take away Allie's seizures, but would always be there with her, even when her mom or another adult couldn't.

The dog would give Rebecca peace of mind.

Which was more than he had at the moment. As he watched the two of them heading his way, he wondered how this one woman and her little girl had managed to get so tangled up in his life. He'd known them less than two weeks, but Rebecca Barnes had managed to establish herself in his waking thoughts and his dreams. He figured that was the last place she'd want to be. And he wasn't so thrilled about it, either.

"Well, are we going in or not?" Lola asked. Her words sounded fuzzy, as she was standing on his left side. He heard that she continued to talk after she asked the question, but Allie was also talking and there were children playing in the church playground.

He turned to give his aunt his good ear. "I didn't catch that."

"Oh, what happened to your head? Did you get tangled up in barbed wire again?" Lola touched his cheek. "Is that infected?"

"No, it isn't infected. Aunt Lola, I didn't hear what you said."

"I don't think it bears repeating. But women like her, they're looking for a wedding ring."

"I think you're wrong on that one, Aunt Lola."

"Mark my words, that gold digger knows you're a wealthy man."

He laughed, even as Rebecca looked somewhat shocked.

"I'm not wealthy and she's not a gold digger."

"You're my only living relative. We don't know if your mother is alive. If she is, I wouldn't give her a dime to call home."

"I don't think there are pay phones anymore, Aunt Lola, and I don't think we should continue this conversation."

She cast a furtive glance around. "The gold digger heard, didn't she?"

"You must be Isaac's aunt Lola," Rebecca said with a big grin on her face. "I'm so glad to meet you."

"Well, at least she has some manners." Lola pumped the hand that Rebecca had extended. "And she's pretty."

"Aunt Lola." He cut his aunt off more sharply than he'd ever done in the past.

"I'm going inside since you obviously don't appreciate my help." She stomped off, but glanced back as she went through the door and gave him a wink. She was trouble, pure and simple. From her braided gray hair and fishing clothes to her old rubber boots.

They entered the building at the side, directly into the fellowship hall. Christmas had arrived. A tree had been decorated and a nativity scene set up on a nearby table. Next to him, Rebecca tensed. Visibly.

He didn't comment. He doubted she wanted his opinion or advice.

Kylie spotted them and headed their way. "Rebecca and Allie, we're glad you could join us. We're still serving dinner. And if Allie would like to join the children, we're going to assign parts for the Christmas program."

"I'm not sure..." Rebecca started. But then she looked down at her daughter and the objections died. "Of course."

Isaac shoved his hands in his pockets and pretended he didn't want to reach for her hand or put an arm around her to comfort her.

Rebecca slipped through the door of the large room where the children were gathered with Kylie and several other adults. She scanned the crowd, spotting Allie in a corner with Jersey and several other girls. They were sitting on the floor, with the dog in the middle of their small group.

Her heart swelled at the sight of her daughter in this setting. It brought back memories of her own childhood in church, and for the first time she regretted that this hadn't been a part of Allie's life. Rebecca had allowed her anger to keep her away from something that had been important to her own formative years.

The rejection, from both her parents and many church members, had hurt. It had cut a deep wound that had obviously not healed well. But there had been good in that little country church. There had been Christmas programs, Sunday potlucks, friends that she still spoke to on occasion.

"You okay?" The deep voice had become familiar to her and she nodded, even as his hand touched her back in a gesture that she was sure he meant as supportive.

"Yes, I'm fine. Just thinking about how much my daughter has missed out on. Not just church, but family. She hasn't spent Christmases with grandparents or had a sleepover with a best friend. All of the little things I took for granted." She let the words spill out, because they'd been held in for too long.

"It's never too late," he told her.

Was it true? That it wasn't too late to give her daughter the circle of love and family she deserved? What would it feel like, to walk back into her parents' lives after everything that had happened?

"I've blamed my parents for a long time. But I own my actions from that summer. I shoved off everything that I knew was right and good for a brief moment in the sun."

"Most people go through that. We have to build our own relationship with God. Our parents' relationship can only take us so far."

"But instead of building a relationship, I burned every bridge between myself and family, myself and God."

"There's still a bridge." He said it softly.

She nodded, agreeing but still unsure. How did a person go back? How did she let go of the hurt, the anger? How did she trust again?

The people who should have been there for her, prayed for her, loved her, had been the ones throwing stones. She still felt the bruises of the words hurled at her by well-meaning church members.

Allie looked up from the circle of friends and spotted them at the door. Suddenly she was heading their way, with Jersey at her side. A big smile lit up her face and her eyes were sparkling with joy.

Rebecca wanted her daughter to always to be this happy, this secure. She swallowed, thinking of Greg. He knew where they were. He would show up. He would want to meet his daughter. Her heart began to race as she considered what that might mean to their safe, happy world.

"Take a deep breath," the man next to her said.

Deep breath. She could do that. Then Allie was there, wrapping her arms around Rebecca and holding on tight.

"I've had so much fun."

"Have you?" Rebecca asked, smiling down at her daughter.

Allie looked up, nodding.

"Mom, did you know there used to be giants on the earth? The Phila…Philistians?" Her nose scrunched as she tried to find the right word.

"Philistines," Rebecca correct.

"Daniel killed one with a stone. Just a slingshot and a stone. That must have taken a lot of faith. What is faith?"

"Faith is the substance of things hoped for, the evidence of things unseen." Isaac spoke the verse, then went down on one knee, his hand settling on Jersey's back. "When you take a deep breath, what do you breathe in?"

"Air," Allie answered.

"Right, oxygen. It's always there. You breathe and you don't even question it. Because you have faith that even though you can't see the air, it's there. And even though we can't see God, we know He is there. And guess when you miss air, or oxygen, the most?"

"If it disappears. But God doesn't disappear, does He?" Allie asked. Her brow furrowed. "Maybe we just stop believing the air is there for us to breathe."

"Maybe," he said.

He rose to his feet again. Allie wasn't finished. She tugged on Rebecca's hand. "I'm going to be an angel in the Christmas program. Do you mind if I'm an angel?"

"Of course I don't mind. You'll make the best angel ever."

Allie studied her face. "You're not going to cry, are you?"

She shook her head. "No, of course not."

"Lean down," Allie demanded.

Rebecca leaned over and Allie studied her eyes. With a small hand she brushed beneath Rebecca's eyes.

"That wasn't a tear," Rebecca insisted.

"It was. It'll be okay, Mom. We have lots of friends here. And no stupid guys that take your money or break your heart."

"What?" Rebecca had never wanted the ground to open up and swallow her more than she did at that moment. "What are you talking about?"

"I heard you talking to your friend Catrina about why you were leaving Arizona."

"You shouldn't have listened." Rebecca sighed. "And I should have been more careful."

"I'll just wait for the two of you out here in the hallway," Isaac said, tipping his hat as he made his escape.

She watched him walk away, then looked at her daughter. "I'm sorry that you heard those conversations."

"I shouldn't have listened. But I'm glad we came here. I like the ranch."

"But the ranch isn't our home. Mr. West has been kind enough to let us stay there until we can find a place of our own."

Allie's crestfallen look for some reason matched what Rebecca felt inside. She claimed to be a grown woman, capable of handling her emotions, but she could admit that she enjoyed living at Mercy Ranch. She liked the people, the wide-open spaces, the smell of country. She didn't want Allie to be disappointed, though.

"Maybe we could pay Mr. West to let us stay?" Allie suggested.

"I don't think it works that way. The ranch is for veterans. That means people who have been in the military, who have fought battles."

"I know what a veteran is, Mom," Allie said with a big-girl voice.

"Yes, of course you do. You know a lot."

"Will we see my grandparents?"

Rebecca nodded. "Yes, eventually."

Kylie approached and looked at the two of them. "Everything okay? Do you mind if we put Allie in the Christmas program?"

"Of course not." Rebecca realized how true the statement was. She felt as if all her broken pieces were coming back together. She'd ignored God for so long, but here was the evidence of things unseen. Even though she'd been ignoring Him, maybe He had been preparing her for this new life.

"Okay, well, then we'll see you next Wednesday. The program won't be difficult but we will practice every Wednesday between now and Christmas and maybe even a couple of Sunday mornings."

"We'll be here," Rebecca assured the other woman. She reached for Allie's hand. "Ready to go?"

Allie took her hand and squeezed it.

Rebecca led her daughter through the now quiet halls. Darkness had fallen and she thought about Greg. About him possibly waiting out there for her. In the dark.

But there were still people around. She wasn't alone.

"I'm so glad I get to be in the program." Allie skipped along next to her. "I'm glad we came to church tonight."

"Me, too."

"Will we come again on Sunday?"

"We might." She walked past the kitchen and someone called out. Jack West waved.

"There are cookies in here if Allie wants one," he offered. She noticed that his voice trembled tonight. It often did in the evenings. She guessed it happened at the end of the day, when he was tired and had worn himself out doing everything he wanted to do.

She nodded for Allie to go on in. "I'll wait here for you. But we have to leave soon, before it gets much later. It's a school night."

Allie skipped away from her, the dog obediently at her side.

"You okay?" Isaac had reappeared.

"Yes, I'm good. I'm sorry, she's nine and filters are optional."

He shrugged. "She's a good kid. I'll walk you out to your car."

"I'd appreciate that."

"How was your first night at church?"

"It wasn't bad," she admitted. "I'm glad we came. I've avoided church because I don't ever want Allie to be hurt the way I was."

"That won't happen here," he assured her. His confidence was maddening.

"How can you know that?" She kept her attention focused on Allie. The child was a social butterfly and had stopped to talk to Jack.

"Because she has you." Isaac bumped his shoulder against hers as he made the statement.

She glanced up at him. His smile took her by surprise. It felt familiar and comforting. And unsettling.

"What do you mean?"

"She has you. Life won't always be easy. Someone somewhere along the way will hurt her, but she'll always have you. And you'll teach her to be strong, to know her self-worth. She'll have you."

The words sank into her heart the way rain soaks into the earth after a long dry spell.

"Thank you," she said, managing to get the words out, and briefly, just briefly, she leaned against him.

For the first time in a long time she didn't remind herself to hold back, to protect her heart. She didn't run through the list of men who had hurt her.

Isaac didn't make false promises. He wasn't promising to be more than he was willing to be. He offered friendship, someone to lean on. That was all.

It had been so long since she'd had those things that she accepted what he offered, even as she told herself to tread carefully where her heart was concerned.

Chapter Nine

Boxes of merchandise and shipments of equipment and supplies began to arrive. By Saturday morning, just a couple weeks since her arrival in Hope, Rebecca was beginning to see that her dream had potential. She thought of Aunt Evelyn and how happy she would have been. They'd had their small salon in Arizona, but the building had been cramped and the location less than ideal.

They'd made a decent living and saved some money.

This shop could become more. Much more. She could see the potential of the space and the location.

And life held promise. She had friends. Allie was healthy. Her parents were a short distance away. Perhaps not exactly accepting, but at least they were nearby if Allie ever needed them.

Would she want Allie to go to them should something ever happen to her? That was a question Rebecca had been dwelling on for a while. No one ever planned on the worst happening, but as a single mom, she had to consider everything.

Jack walked through the front door of the shop. He

was using a cane and had been for the past week. It seemed to give him some stability. She waved and went back to work unpacking the shipment of clothing that had come in. She wanted a small section of the store devoted to trendy clothing and other boutique items. She had ordered jewelry, hair accessories and shoes.

"Where's that girl of yours?" Jack asked.

"In the back room. She's watching television and cuddling with Jersey."

"A girl and her dog," Jack said as he took a seat. "I have a crew finishing breakfast. As soon as they're done, they'll come over and we'll start installing sinks and chairs. How soon do you plan on hiring more stylists? That's what they're called, right? I've always just gone to the barber."

She slipped a top on a hanger and sat back, stretching legs that had been bent for too long.

"If all goes well, I'm hoping to have more people by spring. I know the winter months can be tight, so I'll manage by myself for now." She eyed his sharply cut gray hair. "And you'll have free haircuts for life here."

"Now that's a nice offer. My barber needs to retire. His hand isn't as steady as it was fifty years ago. What if I have a young woman or two interested in going to school to do this?" He waved his hand to indicate the salon and Rebecca smiled.

"I think that would be great as long as I know we can work together."

"I reckon you'd kind of like to hire your own people. Sierra needs to find something she enjoys. I'll pay for her to go to school if you think she would work out for you."

Sierra lived in the women's apartments—the garage,

as they all referred to it. She was working at the resort Jack had reopened in the last year, but she'd shared with Rebecca that she wanted something different. "I think Sierra would be great if it's what she wants to do."

"We'll work on getting her to school. Now, the crew will be here shortly. Don't be shy. Just tell them what you need."

She pushed herself to her feet and hugged him. "Jack, I can't tell you how much I appreciate your help."

"I'm glad I could do this," he replied. "When I got sober all of those years ago, I never realized this would be my path. I thought I'd get sober, run my ranch and be a little better person than I'd been for twenty or thirty years. You never know what lies ahead of you."

She frowned at those sage words. When she was a little girl, she'd dreamed of her "someday," when she would be married, have a few kids. Back then she'd thought she'd be a teacher. Or maybe run a day care.

Jack was right; people never knew where their path might lead them.

The door opened and several of the men from the ranch entered. She hadn't expected to see Isaac, but there he was in the middle of the group. Her day got a little brighter, seeing him, all cowboyed up in his faded jeans and a button-up flannel shirt. He lifted a plastic bag that held a couple of take-out containers.

"Did you eat breakfast?" he asked as he approached.

"I had something," she hedged.

"A slice of toast with spray-on butter," he admonished. "I brought a chicken biscuit with gravy. And pancakes for Allie. No doubt she had cereal, but I know she'd eat again."

Rebecca started to object, to tell him he didn't have

to do this. It wouldn't have been honest. She could smell whatever wonderful thing was in that container and she wanted it. He pulled it out of her reach.

"No fair," she said.

He started to move it back, but stopped and wobbled, reaching quickly to steady himself. His hand landed on her arm. "Well, that's not how I planned this."

"I was just told that nothing ever goes exactly the way we plan."

"Been talking to Jack?" Isaac asked, after taking a deep breath.

"Of course she has," Jack answered for her. "She's a smart lady."

"Because she listens to you?"

"Well, of course," his dad retorted.

Isaac shook his head. "You're too much."

Jack stood, the cane he'd been using held lightly in his hand. He winked at his son. "Isaac, you have a lot to learn."

Allie and Jersey came running from the back room, saving the day for Rebecca. Her daughter's presence took away the uncomfortable feeling that had started to build between them.

"Isaac, you're here! Did you know there's a float in the parade next weekend?"

"I did know that. I helped build it. And since you're an angel in the program, you'll have to be in the parade, too."

She hugged him hard. "I've never been in a parade. Will you be on the float with us?"

"No, I'll be riding a horse."

"Which one?" she asked. "I'd like to ride a horse. I'm not sure if angels can do that."

"I think angels have to stay on the float. But we'll get you on a horse soon."

"What's in the bag?" Allie forgot the parade and stuck her nose in the plastic bag.

"I'm pretty sure there's an order of pancakes and a carton of chocolate milk," he answered. "Are you hungry?"

"Always," Allie said. She waited, not quite patiently, as he pulled the container from the bag.

"Say thank you," Rebecca reminded her.

"Thank you, Isaac." She took the container and her dog and headed for the back room again. "I'm going to watch the surfer girl movie."

"Okay," Rebecca called out to a child who'd already disappeared.

She became aware of the work crew, whose presence she'd forgotten. They were moving sinks into place, giving her the first glimpse of her salon. Tears misted her eyes as she glanced around the place. Then her gaze collided with Isaac's.

"It's too much," she said. Too much happening in such a short amount of time.

Too much to have her daughter getting attached to Isaac. He might say that he wasn't good with children, that kids weren't his thing. But he made Allie feel safe. He made her laugh.

Isaac looked around at the work taking place. "It isn't too much."

Of course he didn't think so. He was at the center of the "too much." Because he was so easy to like. She'd had her heart broken by men in the past. Including her own father.

She'd never had a man for a friend. If something

happened between them, she knew it would hurt even more than being cheated on, or dumped.

Isaac opened her meal and held it in front of her. "I'm going to let you have this. I would never keep it from you."

She shook her head and accepted the offering. He deserved an explanation. "Thank you for being a friend. I definitely didn't expect that when you stumbled into my car a few weeks ago."

"I didn't stumble into your car."

"You definitely did."

He kissed the top of her head. "Becca, you clearly need friends if you're thanking me for being one."

"I'm not that pathetic. I do have friends." She took a bite of the chicken biscuit, making sure to get extra gravy. "I've just never had one bring me a chicken biscuit with gravy. I don't want it to go to your head, but that gives you a place at the top."

"Only because you don't know me very well. I'm going to help the guys install the sinks, then I have to get back to the ranch and work some horses." Suddenly something shifted, changed in his eyes. His smile evaporated.

She'd gone too far, she realized. He could handle friendship, but he was the type to turn tail and run if he thought a woman wanted more. If it wouldn't have seemed pathetic, she'd have assured him she wanted nothing more than friendship.

Even if that wasn't exactly the truth.

Isaac rode the dun horse, Pepper, into the indoor arena. He'd been working hard since leaving Rebecca and the salon. He'd called her Becca. But he didn't have the right to give her a nickname.

She was a single mom with a daughter. The last thing she needed was a casual friendship. Or even a casual date. He knew better. He'd prayed to make better decisions now than he'd made in his younger years. He'd prayed, really prayed, that God would just make him happy to be single.

Because the truth was, he'd always wanted a family. A wife. Kids. A home. Sunday dinners after church, school programs, handprints traced on paper hanging on the fridge. It wasn't a dream most men admitted to. Not when their friends were talking about clubbing on Saturday nights, and the latest woman they'd been dating.

"Hold steady," he said to Joe, who had agreed to help him work the dun by getting on a horse. Joe hated riding. Which was too bad, because he was a decent rider for a guy living his life as an amputee.

"Hold steady he says," Joe grumbled. "Sierra, bring your horse in a little closer. The boss wants us to hold steady."

Sierra had been at the ranch for two years, and she'd kept to herself until about six months ago. The horses were slowly but surely bringing her into the group, and out of her shell.

Isaac managed to catch most of what his friend had said. "I heard that."

"I meant for you to hear it. I think you're riding to relieve stress and we're collateral damage."

"Yep, that's it." He held the dun steady. The horse eyed the steer and then went to work, right, left, right, left, backing up and then shifting quickly to the right again to keep the steer from moving past them.

He let the steer move past, back to the herd, and then he cut another one from the tightly clustered group. He moved the animal to the center of the arena away from the others.

The dun moved easily. A tap of Isaac's boot on the right side made the horse swing to the left. A tap on his left side made him move to the right. He had a few bad habits, but nothing Isaac couldn't work out of him. Sometimes he kept moving backward when he was supposed to come to a quick stop. And he didn't always respond to leg commands.

"He's a decent horse," Sierra called out, as she kept the steer from running past her.

"Yeah, I think he's going to do well. I have a buyer for him."

"Hey, Rebecca, how are you?" Joe said, a little too cheerfully. He stopped his horse and headed toward the edge of the arena.

Isaac shot a glance over his shoulder and saw that she was there, watching them. He caught Sierra's look, the moment when she rolled her eyes.

He ignored her. If he denied anything she would say that only proved his guilt.

"Do you want to work your horse on his leads while we're out here?" He asked because he knew he'd been standing there like a fool.

She shook her head. "Nah, I think we're good."

"He's keeping his head down?" he asked, because the horse she rode had a tendency to toss his head. He'd put a tie-down on the gelding, a strap that ran from the underside of the bridle to the breast collar.

"Yeah, now that he's used to the tie-down. Go talk to her."

"Next week try him without the tie-down and see if he keeps his head down. We don't want him knocking you under the chin."

She grinned at that. "No, no one wants to be taken by surprise."

"You can go now," he said.

She saluted and rode out of the arena. Joe had already left. He was standing next to Rebecca, his horse behind him, lipping Rebecca's blond hair. She brushed his muzzle away and then slid a hand down his copper-penny-colored neck.

Isaac ignored the strange tension inside him. It didn't matter that Joe was flirting with her. It didn't matter that he wanted to be the only man she smiled at. It mattered that she needed to be safe. And he didn't feel like the man who could be that for a woman. He could protect her, should Allie's father show up. Or at least he hoped he could.

But that's as far as he would take this, whatever *this* was.

Joe saw him coming, said something Isaac couldn't hear. The cheerful look on his face spoke volumes, but Isaac still wished he could have heard what the other man had said to her. Whatever it was, she laughed and avoided looking at Isaac.

Until he was right in front of her, dismounting as his horse moved to the right. Once his feet were on the ground, he pulled the animal close.

"I haven't seen a cutting horse work cattle in a long time," Rebecca said.

He turned a bit, giving her his good ear.

"Where's Allie?" he asked, as he pushed the dun's head away.

"She's staying with Kylie and Carson. They're having a sleepover with Allie, their two children and a girl from church who is Allie's age." Rebecca looked lost. "She's never been away from me overnight before."

"She'll be fine with Kylie and Carson, you know."

"Probably," she agreed.

"Let's go for a ride." The suggestion was spontaneous. "It's getting close to sunset and on a cool night like tonight, with just the right amount of clouds, it should be spectacular. I'll make us a thermos of coffee and we can head for the pond."

He'd gone from offering a ride to distract her to offering the most romantic thing his cowboy brain could think of. He knew most men would offer dinner, flowers, maybe jewelry. But for him, a ride across Oklahoma hill country at sunset was at the top of the list. She probably wouldn't agree.

Hopefully, her mind wasn't on romance, because his shouldn't be heading in that direction. He didn't know what it was about this woman that made him want to shove all those convictions of his in a vault.

One good nightmare and he'd remember why this was a bad idea. Memories of Jack drinking to forget the pain of war. A path Isaac prayed he'd never take.

But he'd been tempted. After his injury, when they'd given him pills, he'd been tempted. He'd soon realized that the pills had become a problem.

Carson had recently told him that awareness meant he wasn't like Jack.

"I'm not sure," she said after a minute.

"It would take your mind off worrying about Allie." She'd almost said no and here he was, trying to lure her back to yes.

With any other woman he wouldn't worry about a ride at sunset. Because he wouldn't want there to be a second ride. But Rebecca tempted a guy to think about spending more time in her presence.

"I haven't ridden in years."

"It's like riding a bike," he said encouragingly.

"Okay, but I have to change."

"You're fine. There are boots in the office. Probably a pair that fits. We don't want to miss that sunset."

Suddenly, seeing the sunset with her was the most important thing in his life.

He left her in the office to find a pair of boots and wait on the coffee to perk so she could pour it into a thermos.

"I'm adding sugar and cream," she informed him as he walked out the office door.

"I'm a man who can admit he likes his coffee sweet," he replied, not bothering to hide the smile that her easy banter brought on.

He picked a gentle mare named Dolly for her. A pretty buckskin with a sweet disposition and a smooth gait. The mare was saddled and ready to go when Rebecca walked out of the office with a thermos of coffee and a couple snack cakes.

"I like sweet coffee, but no thanks to the junk food."

She gave him a casual look. "No junk?"

"Nope. Too many additives. I've found they make the headaches worse."

She turned away from him as she said something. He saw her lips move but didn't quite catch the words.

He put a hand on her arm and brought her back around to face him. "I didn't hear that."

Her cheeks turned pink. "I'm sorry."

"It's okay. I don't want to miss anything important. Like if you tell me I'm amazing and I don't respond, you'll think I didn't care."

"If I tell you that you think too highly of yourself, I want to make sure you don't miss a word."

"Yeah, that, too." He took the coffee and snack cakes and put them in the saddlebag on his horse. "Let me introduce you to Dolly."

He took her hand and led her to the buckskin. Dolly had a soft gold coat and black mane and tail. Her eyes were as gentle as her personality.

"She's beautiful," Rebecca said, stroking her hand down the horse's neck.

"She was a rescue. She came to us half-starved and cut up. She's a great horse for the men and women on the ranch. We use her for lessons and for therapy."

He watched as Rebecca leaned in close to the horse. "She's perfect."

Dolly cuddled into the woman who was giving her plenty of attention, petting her face and whispering in her big ears. Isaac had never thought of himself as the jealous type, but...

"We should go," he said, untying his horse. "We'll mount up outside. You'll be warm enough?"

"It isn't that cold," she told him as she untied the mare. "It has been a change for us, getting used to the colder weather."

They mounted up in the small corral to the side of the barn and he opened the gate to let them through. She seemed to know what she was doing, holding the reins comfortably as if it hadn't been years since she'd ridden.

Dolly perked up, her ears twitching, probably happy

with the lighter weight of a female. One who obviously knew how to ride.

Isaac nudged the dun forward and rode alongside her.

"Where are we going?" she asked, keeping her gaze between her horse's ears.

He'd purposely put himself on her left so that he wouldn't miss anything she said. He pointed toward the pond in the distance. Already the red-and-orange glow of the setting sun reflected on the dark water.

"It's beautiful." Rebecca spoke softly. Dolly's ears twitched again.

"It is. There's a small rise just past the pond. It's the best view."

She nodded, looking toward the hill he'd indicated. "I guess you do this often?"

"Usually by myself, but yeah. I enjoy church, but this is where I feel God's presence most."

She shot him a look, not quite disbelieving, but there was some doubt. He knew she was still trying to wrap her mind around trusting God. After what she'd been through, he understood that.

"It isn't that I doubt your faith," she said, as if she read his thoughts. They were probably written all over his face.

"Okay."

She started again. "I don't doubt your faith. I just didn't expect it."

He grinned. "Because I'm such a good-looking cowboy?"

She laughed. "Well, it isn't as if you have the market on humility cornered. And I don't know, maybe that's part of it. Or maybe I haven't met many men who were actually living their faith."

"I think you've been meeting the wrong men," he told her as they passed the pond. The sun was sinking toward the western horizon now. He glanced at the woman riding next to him. "Ready for a lope?"

She nodded and they nudged their horses forward at an easy pace, covering the ground a little quicker than the sedate walk of earlier. He heard her laugh, the sound carrying on the wind. He chanced a look at her, honey-blond hair blowing back and pale cheeks rosy with the wind and the cold.

She was beautiful. He had known that since the day she showed up in town, but it struck him full force in a way that wouldn't let a man take a deep breath. He shook his head and nearly lost his hat. He pushed it down on his head and brought his horse around, slowing to walk to the top of the hill.

Dolly closed the gap between them as he turned and brought the gelding to a stop. The sun was dipping below the horizon and there were just enough clouds to paint the sky in lavender, pink, orange and violet. The colors reflected on the pond. Somewhere in the distance a coyote howled.

Isaac pulled the coffee out of the saddlebag and poured the caramel-colored brew into the plastic cap. He offered it to her first. She took it and sipped, then handed it back. It was still hot, had just the right amount of sugar, and sharing it felt too intimate. But he felt, deep down, that this mattered.

She mattered. In a way that he couldn't explain. He'd never want to hurt her. He didn't want to wake up someday and realize he'd hurt her during a nightmare, or that the addiction he feared would creep up on him.

He had a hard enough time being responsible for his own life without adding other people to the mix.

They emptied the coffee cup and he refilled it as she reached into the saddlebag and pulled out a snack cake. She offered one of the squares to him. It was tempting to take that piece of white cake, but he shook his head.

"No, I'd better not." He always said the same thing each time someone offered him a drink of alcohol. Since addiction ran in his family, it was best to avoid it altogether.

The sun sank lower and the colors faded, washed away by the dark blue of early evening. He pointed to the south.

Her eyes widened. "Christmas lights?"

"You can see Hope from here. The town display is up. And people are starting to decorate."

"It's beautiful." She had a wide-eyed look of wonder on her face, as if it were her first Christmas. He guessed in a way it was. Her first Christmas back in Oklahoma. The first in which she might be finding faith again.

"You have it all wrong," he told her.

Her eyes narrowed. "Wrong?"

"The lights are pretty. *You're* beautiful."

She started to object.

"You're beautiful," he repeated, as he leaned closer. He slid his hand to the back of her neck, where soft tresses of blond hair caressed his skin.

Her lips parted and he kissed her tenderly, tasting the sweetness of the cake on her lips. She touched his arm and, as she drew back, whispered his name.

"Becca, we have a serious problem."

"Yes, we do."

"I'm determined not to hurt you, but I'm afraid a relationship with me would, in time, do so. And if I hurt you, I hurt Allie. I wouldn't want to do that, either."

"I've taken too many chances with my heart, with my daughter's heart. I trust you, Isaac. I don't trust myself. And I also know that we're not on the same page where our faith is concerned and that will matter. Maybe not right now, but eventually."

"So we stop now before we're in too deep?" he said, as he headed his horse in the direction of the barn, Rebecca riding next to him.

"I think so."

"I'd like to be your friend," he told her, as darkness fell over them. "Just friends. No more kisses in the moonlight."

"No more setting suns." She nudged her horse into an easy trot.

He nodded. "No more setting suns."

It should be simple. They hadn't known each other that long. They were pretty decent friends already. So why complicate things? Even as he told himself it should be easy, Isaac found himself missing her. He was already missing all the sunsets they wouldn't watch together. All the coffee they wouldn't share. He knew he was doing the right thing, keeping their relationship platonic, but it sure didn't feel right.

Chapter Ten

"You're going to church?" Eve asked as she entered the kitchen the women shared.

Rebecca nodded as she took a sip of her coffee. And tried not to think about sharing coffee with Isaac. It had been intimate, something that changed things between them. The coffee. Watching that sunset together. It had been more than just the kiss.

Eve gave her a discerning look as she dropped a couple slices of bread in the toaster. "Did you eat?"

"No, but I'm good. Do you want coffee?"

Eve pulled a cup off the rack on the counter. "I'd love a cup. I guess we can't convince you to stay on the ranch? I'm going to miss you."

Rebecca slid the cup across the counter. Eve drank her coffee black. And strong.

"For now I'm here. I'm sure I'll eventually find a place. But I don't want to take a spot at the ranch that someone else might need."

Eve backed her wheelchair up and grabbed peanut butter out of a lower cabinet. "We've got plenty of room."

Rebecca watched the woman. With her dark hair, equally dark eyes and careful but cheerful smile, she was fast becoming a friend.

"Will you leave at some point?" Rebecca asked Eve. In retrospect, the question felt intrusive. "I'm sorry, that's none of my business."

"You don't have to apologize. It's a question I ask myself from time to time. I have family in Texas. But Mercy Ranch is my home now. I'm not sure I'd want to leave."

"I can understand that. It's easy to make this place a home. I don't want Allie to get attached and then have to leave."

"Yeah, it's hard for a kid. They always say that kids adjust. But as a child who moved a lot, I think it's more a saying than a reality. New schools, new homes, new friends. After a while it got easier not to have friends."

It was a brief glimpse into the woman's life, her careful smiles and guarded attitude.

"I grew up in the same house, going to the same school." Rebecca wanted to give Eve something because she felt the other woman had shared a bit of herself she didn't usually. "I used to trust too easily. Now I feel it's a lot safer to keep my distance. I have to protect my heart and my daughter."

"Is that why you..." Eve shook her head. "Sorry. I went too far. You ready to go to church? Did you say Kylie and Carson are bringing Allie? I have to admit, I missed her last night."

"So did I. We've never been apart overnight."

"You're a good mom, Rebecca."

They left together, Eve riding with her. As they drove past the main house, Jack stepped out with Isaac, who helped his father make his unsteady way to the waiting truck.

"Jack is getting worse," Eve said softly. "A year ago he was still strong and going nonstop. It's hard to see him like this."

She didn't say more. Rebecca wondered if there were people in Eve's life who might have a hard time seeing her as someone other than the person they'd once known. Maybe that's why she stayed on the ranch rather than going home to Texas.

They arrived at the church several minutes early. The SUV Carson and Kylie drove was already there. Rebecca parked and got out. She hurried to help Eve get her chair out of the back. The other woman transferred herself and grabbed her purse.

"Ready to go," Eve said. She peered up at Rebecca. "You look as if I'm taking you into a torture chamber."

"The last time I was in church, it fit that description."

"Bad experience?" Eve asked, as she navigated the parking lot.

"Want me to help?" Rebecca offered.

"If you don't mind… I can usually get around, but sometimes there's a rough patch."

"I never know if I should ask."

"Don't worry about it. I'm never offended if someone offers help."

She grabbed the handles of the chair and got Eve up on the sidewalk.

"Thanks. I can take it from here. Now, about the bad church experience…"

"My dad was the pastor. When I was eighteen I rebelled. I got pregnant and didn't want them to know. Allie's father convinced me we should steal the offerings from church and take off for California. In the end I gave the money back, but my father dragged me before the congregation and listed my many sins. I publicly apologized, then he put me on a bus for Arizona."

"Wow." Eve stopped her chair. "That's tough. You were just a kid."

"I know. I can't imagine ever doing that to my daughter."

"People do it, though." Eve shrugged and replaced her hands on the wheels of the chair. "I think it cuts deeper when our wounds happen in church."

"Yeah, I guess that might be true. So here I am, and I'm not sure if I want to walk through those doors."

They could hear children singing inside. Eve glanced back. "I think you're going to want to go in there and see your daughter practicing for the Christmas program. People are human, they're real, they make real mistakes. But I think this church, the people here, are genuinely good. They do their best."

"Thank you." Rebecca gripped the handles of Eve's chair and pushed it up the ramp.

And inside she saw her daughter standing on the stage, quoting a Bible verse. "'For unto you is born this day in the city of David, a savior who is Christ the Lord.'"

The angels began to sing. Rebecca closed her eyes and listened, picking out her daughter's voice.

The service that day was a blur. It mattered only that she'd seen Allie on the stage with the other children. She'd been happy and healthy, her dog nearby. Even angels needed a little help from time to time.

Rebecca had survived her first day back in church. She'd witnessed joy on her child's face. She knew, beyond a shadow of a doubt, that she'd made the right choice moving here. And she was so thankful to Jack for the opportunity he'd given her.

After the service, she stood at the periphery of the group of Wests and the inhabitants of the ranch as they all made lunch plans, discussed the service and talked about the unseasonably warm day. Isaac moved to her side.

"What are your plans for the rest of the day?" he asked.

"I have to run by the salon. I need to put some things up and make sure everything is ready tomorrow, when they install the pedicure chairs."

"We can take Allie with us to the ranch," Eve offered. "I'm riding with Sierra, so you can go take care of things."

"That would be nice. I'd hate for her to sit around and wait for me. I should only be thirty minutes or so."

"We'll keep an eye on her." Eve motioned for Allie to join her. "You're going to ride with us so your mom can get some work done. Is that okay?"

"Yeah, that'll be fun." Allie held her dog close. "Come on, Jersey."

Off she went. As if she didn't mind leaving her mother behind. It was good, Rebecca told herself. It was a natural part of a child growing up.

"Don't look so stricken," Isaac whispered in her ear. "She'll see your face and then she won't want to go."

She nodded. "You're right."

"You're giving her wings, Becca. That's what you're supposed to do."

She wanted to hug him, but she wouldn't. They were friends, nothing more.

He walked her to her car. "I'm not sure if you should go to the salon alone."

"I thought you're giving me wings," she teased.

"Right. Of course. But don't…"

"Talk to strangers? Don't worry, I'm fine."

She got in her car and he closed the door. Then he waved to her as she backed out of her parking space.

It was only a few blocks from the church to the salon on Lakeside Drive. The streets were one-way, so she had to drive down Second Street to the highway, back around and down Lakeside. When she pulled up to her shop, another car pulled in next to her. She already had the door open and was stepping out when the other driver got out and she realized her mistake.

Greg was ten years older. His hair had thinned and there was gray at the temples. His face was sunken in and he was pale. How had she ever been attracted to this man? He hadn't been kind, even then. He'd used her. He'd laughed at her.

What in the world had she wanted at eighteen that she thought this man could give her? Stupid. She'd been so stupid. So naive.

"Don't you look pretty? It's been a long time, Becca. I thought you'd at least write to me, considering I robbed that store in order to give you a better life."

"Go away, Greg."

"I wish I could. Thing is—" he grinned "—I want to see Allie. Maybe I'll take you to court and get custody of her."

"I don't—" No. Arguing with him would only spur his anger. She didn't want him angry. She wanted him gone. "I have to go. I'll talk to a lawyer about visits."

He leaned on his car, leering at her. "You think that's what I want. I don't want visits. I want weekends."

"I see."

"I heard you came into some money when your aunt passed away."

Ah, so that was his game. It always came back to money with him.

"I put my money into this salon. But she didn't leave much." Another worthless man had already beaten him to her savings. Men were always taking from her.

No more. Now she was in charge of her future.

"I bet you could come up with some money. I looked inside that fancy shop of yours. You've spent some serious money on that equipment. Maybe that rancher guy you're living with could cough up some money, too. I bet he has extra cash in a drawer somewhere."

"I'm not breaking the law for you, Greg. You'll have to go now."

"That's what I'm trying to do, you stupid…"

She froze him with a glare. "Don't talk to me that way."

"Or you'll what? Keep me from my daughter? You've already done that. I need money to leave the state. I'm not going back to prison."

"You should call your parole officer."

"Gee, thanks for the advice." He stared at her for a minute, and she thought he would leave, but then he started toward her. "Let me give you some advice. Don't mess with me. I'll make you regret it."

Rebecca pushed away from him as he grabbed her. His arms went around her and he pulled, grasping her left arm as he yanked her closer. His grip tightened, but she pushed her free hand into his nose, knocking him back just enough to get away.

She managed to get in her car and lock the door before he regained his footing and came after her again. She backed out of the parking space, not caring that she almost hit him.

Adrenaline pumped through her body as she drove the few miles to the ranch. By the time she parked at the apartment, her entire body trembled and she couldn't catch her breath.

Then she saw Allie. Riding a horse.

She jumped out of the car and tore across the lawn toward the corral, where Allie sat atop Dolly.

"No!" she shouted to Isaac, who waved, as if he'd done nothing wrong.

"Stop." She brushed at her wet cheeks, shaking inside. She had to get control of herself. "Get her off that horse. Now."

Isaac climbed the fence and dropped down in front of her. His hands gripped her arms, gently but firmly. He made eye contact with her, his face scrunching as he studied her.

"Calm down."

"She'll fall. She'll have a seizure and fall off the horse. What if she…"

"She isn't going to fall. I'm right here."

But Rebecca hadn't been there. Her heart was shattering and she didn't even know why. She breathed in, trying not to fall apart in front of her daughter. Isaac moved, blocking Allie's view. She heard her daughter call out, asking if she could see that she was riding a horse.

Rebecca nodded, but couldn't answer.

* * *

Isaac held on to Rebecca, who appeared to be falling apart right in front of him. He glanced back at her daughter, still circling the corral on Dolly. Jersey sat a short distance away.

"I think it's time to end this riding lesson," he called out.

He spotted Sierra coming out of the barn. She headed their way, eyes widening when she noticed Rebecca.

"Can you get Allie?" Isaac asked. "Tell her Rebecca and I have to discuss something about the shop. Maybe get her some ice cream. Or show her some of the tricks Jersey knows. I haven't taught her the good ones yet."

"Sure thing, Isaac." Sierra put a hand on Rebecca's shoulder. "Do you need me?"

She shook her head, but her eyes were wide, troubled.

"Becca, let's go talk." Isaac started her toward the barn, but she drew back.

"Don't call me that. Don't *ever* call me that."

Fear crept in, taking him by surprise. He reached for her hand. "I'll never call you that again."

He noticed the bruises, but obviously caused by someone holding her arm tight. Fear turned to rage.

"What happened?"

"Not here," she whispered.

He held her hand gently and guided her through the barn to the office. "Water?"

She nodded as she took a seat. She drew a deep breath and started sobbing. "I didn't expect this."

"Was it Greg?"

She nodded, accepting the bottle of water he'd opened for her. She took a sip.

"He hurt you." Isaac managed to say the words without sounding as angry as he felt.

"He followed me to the shop. At first he pretended he wanted to see Allie. And then he started in about money. I thought he would leave, but he came at me. I should have known better."

"I shouldn't have let you go there alone. You won't be there alone again until he's caught."

"What if they don't catch him?" She looked up, her brown eyes luminous in the dimly lit office.

"They'll catch him. We need to call the police. You have to file charges against him. The more they have on him, the better."

"I just want him to go away."

"I know."

She drank a few sips of water. "I need to go to Allie. She'll know something is wrong. And I don't want to be away from her."

"You can't smother her."

Her head popped up, those luminous brown eyes now flashing all the fire of a protective mother.

"She's my daughter. And I don't want her on a horse."

"Because…?"

"She could have a seizure."

"So you'll keep her in a bubble her entire life because she *might* have a seizure? Rebecca, I was right there with her. I wouldn't let anything happen to her. She's a little girl who wants to have normal little-girl experiences."

She covered her face with her hands and he went to her, sitting on the edge of the desk and debating if it would be wise to take her in his arms.

"Rebecca, I know how it is to feel alone. I know how

hard it is to trust. I was an angry kid. I was an even angrier teenager. It took a lot of God to get me to the point that I forgave. I had to forgive my mom for walking out on me. I had to forgive my dad, Jack. I had stuff I had to forgive myself for. I was full of myself, didn't show a lot of respect to the women I dated. I wasn't always the nicest guy."

She dimpled at that. But she didn't say anything.

"I was not the guy I would want anyone's daughter to date."

"Stop. I trust you," she interjected. He was glad, because he didn't want to tell her any more of his stories. "I never expected to find this place. I certainly didn't expect you to make us feel like a part of your family. But you have. And I don't want to bring all of my troubles down on Jack or you or the people on the ranch."

"You think we can't handle trouble? Before Kylie and Carson got married, she had a guy so riled he attacked her at the hospital after Jack had a heart attack. We're used to trouble. And we're not afraid of it."

"I'm afraid of Greg," she admitted in a quiet voice. "Not of what he might do to me. I'm afraid he'll hurt Allie."

"We won't let him," Isaac reassured her.

"Do I tell Allie about him, about Greg? I can't really call him her father. He's never been that." She exhaled loudly, as if the weight of the world was in that sigh.

"I don't know," Isaac admitted, frustrated because he couldn't just fix it all for them.

"I know, and I'm sorry for putting you on the spot. He knows we're staying here."

"Yeah, I figured he would find out. We'll all be watching for him. We won't leave you or Allie alone."

"I should go. Maybe I should find a place to rent? Or go to Tulsa and stay with my friend Carleen?"

"Run from him?"

She shrugged, one shoulder lifting beneath her pale blue sweater. "I don't know what else to do. I feel like he's going to ruin everything. One way or another he's going to tear apart everything we're building here."

"I think you're building your faith. He can't take that. We won't let him take anything else."

"Thank you, Isaac. I'm not sure what I would do without you, without your friendship."

Yeah, friendship. He swallowed a lump that was half guilt and half regret. It got lodged somewhere near his heart.

"You were upset when I called you Becca." He needed to know why.

"That's what Greg always called me. Seeing him today, it shook me and brought back things I'd forgotten about him."

"I won't call you that again, I promise." He hopped down from his desk and, after a slight hesitation, kissed the top of her head. Her hand squeezed his.

"It's okay."

It wasn't. He wanted to hurt this guy, Greg. Badly. "Does Greg have a last name?"

"Baxter."

"Got it. I'm going to call the police now."

"Okay. I know we have to. Would it be okay if I went to the house for a minute to check on Allie? I need to hug her."

"Go ahead. I'll make the call and ask them if we can meet them in town. That way Allie won't see."

Before she left, Rebecca stood on tiptoe and kissed

his cheek. "I'm glad I gave you a ride, cowboy. I didn't know how much I needed a friend."

Yeah, a friend. He held a smile on his face until she walked out the door. He'd never expected all this with her to be so complicated. But she was. Because before, he'd been able to keep women at a distance. He'd had female friends. Kylie. Eve. Sierra. Countless others.

Rebecca was more. In every way that counted, she was more. And that made him want to protect her. From Greg. From himself. She deserved some nice, uncomplicated guy who didn't have a ton of baggage. A guy who didn't have nightmares that sometimes turned violent.

What he wouldn't give to be the type of guy she truly deserved.

Chapter Eleven

The little girl laughed as she opened the package containing the doll. She hugged the soldiers who had given it to her and then ran off down the street into the dusky Afghan evening. As she ran away, he realized she no longer had dark hair. She had blond hair. He screamed her name. Allie! The explosion rocked the ground and the girl disappeared.

He sat up straight in bed. The darkness of his room enveloped him. He leaned forward, wiping at the perspiration on his forehead. It took a minute to catch his breath, to realize he was in Oklahoma, and that Allie was safe.

Joe, on the other hand, wasn't. He was leaning against the wall, a hand on his cheek. He wiggled his chin and muttered something about a strong right hook.

"I hit you?" Isaac brushed a palm down his face. "Man, I'm so sorry."

"It must have been some nightmare."

"The worst. The little girl turned into Allie."

"You know that's not possible, right?"

Isaac jerked on his boots and grabbed a jacket. "Of

course I know that. I'm going to start locking my door at night so you can't come in here and try to wake me up. One of these days I might really hurt you."

"One of these days the dreams might end," Joe said. "Look, we both have sleepless nights. It isn't as if you're waking me up out of a sound sleep and it isn't like I can't handle myself. It was barely a tap on the cheek."

"Now you're just insulting me," Isaac told the other man. "I'm going for a walk."

He headed out the front door, the cold air taking his breath. It was exactly what he needed to clear his mind. The dream had shaken him deeply.

But the girl in the dream turning to Allie—that was the real nightmare. As he walked, Maximus joined him. Someone else was up early. Eve had probably let the dog out.

"What's the matter, Max, couldn't sleep?" He stopped, breathing in the cool, late fall air. It was autumn for only two more weeks; then it would officially be winter.

He didn't care about official dates. The weather was pure winter. The clouds had that heavy look of snow and the air felt damp with humidity. He buttoned his jacket as he walked. Looking down was a mistake, though. When he raised his head, the world spun a little.

He waited for things to settle, then he continued his walk. The main house was lit up and he the smell of bacon wafted on the breeze, luring him in that direction. From inside the house he could hear music. Maria, he guessed, would have arrived already. She would be fixing breakfast, starting the day's chores. He could sure handle breakfast that someone else cooked.

As he stepped through the back door the aromas of cinnamon and bacon greeted him. He wiped his boots on the rug in the utility porch and hung his hat on the rack next to the door. He could hear voices in the kitchen. Maria and someone else, a soft and familiar voice. He reached for his hat, thinking it might be better if he left. He wasn't sure he wanted to see Rebecca, not with his emotions so raw after his dream.

"My mom made cinnamon rolls." A younger voice piped up behind him.

"You really should stop sneaking up on people."

Allie grinned at his warning. "You should pay more attention. Is it because you couldn't hear me?"

"Yeah, and I was focused on something else." He looked away, not wanting to relive the dream.

He obviously wasn't going to escape. She stayed right with him as he took off his coat.

"What are you doing up so early?" he asked.

"My mom promised me cinnamon rolls. And I have school today. Miss Kylie is picking me up. Mom is going to try to open the salon for part of the day."

"Is she really?" He headed into the kitchen, the nine-year-old jabbering about cinnamon rolls and Jersey.

They were already part of the Mercy Ranch family, she and her mother. That's the way it was with the ranch, with Jack and the people he took in. Isaac told himself it was that simple. It wasn't because Rebecca was getting under his skin. It certainly wasn't because Allie should be someone's daughter. Someone ought to be there to look out for the two of them, take them to church. Someone. But not him. Definitely not Greg.

"Yeah, she's excited. She said because it's Monday, more people might be in town. And even though everything isn't ready, people might come in."

"That's a great idea."

"Hey, what are you two up to?" Rebecca asked, as they entered the kitchen together.

"Talking about you opening your salon today." Isaac gave her a questioning look that she wouldn't answer, not with Allie right there.

In his opinion, she shouldn't be there alone. But he realized a friend's opinion didn't count for much.

"I thought, no time like the present."

"Yeah, I guess that's true. What's Maria cooking up?"

"Bacon and eggs and toast, Isaac," Maria called out from her place at the stove. She didn't bother looking at him. "Do you need some tea?"

"Afraid so."

"Thought that might be why you were here so early and not at the barn. Or you smelled my bacon cooking."

"Both." He avoided making eye contact with Rebecca.

Maria wiped her hands on a towel and grabbed the teakettle. "The tea is in the usual place in the cabinet, above the toaster."

"Got it." He pulled the jar out.

"Okay, I'll get the water going. You know how to make the tea. And breakfast is ready. I'm going to do some laundry."

"Thanks, Maria."

"You're welcome." She patted his cheek before she turned to leave. "Oh, if you don't mind, I need some outside decorations put up. The wreath for the front door, twinkle lights and the outdoor nativity scene."

"I don't mind at all. It might have to wait a few hours."

"Of course."

He glanced at the food Maria had placed in warming trays on the counter. It would be there for any of the men who came in looking for breakfast. He realized he wasn't as ready to eat as he'd thought, so he bypassed the main dishes and grabbed a slice of toast.

The teakettle whistled and Rebecca got to it first, pouring boiling water into the cup that held the herbal tea Kylie kept on hand for him.

"This smells so good. What is it?" she asked, as the tea steeped.

"Peppermint, feverfew, chamomile and I'm not sure what else." He inhaled the scent from the brew. "But I've never thought of it as good."

"Have a seat. I'll finish it up for you." Rebecca pointed to a chair at the island. "You don't look so great."

"Thanks," he said.

A car honked outside. He glanced at the clock. "It's awfully early for school."

"Carson is taking the kids out to breakfast at the café."

"And missing out on cinnamon rolls?" Isaac teased.

Allie hugged him, taking him by surprise. "Feel better."

"Thanks, Allie." He smoothed a hand down the back of her head. "You're okay. Even if you are always sneaking up on me."

She laughed. "I think you're okay, too. You're like a dad."

His heart thudded hard and he glanced up to find Rebecca watching, a stricken expression on her face. Allie didn't notice their looks or the awkward silence. She'd dropped that bombshell, grabbed her backpack and lunch box and hurried out the back door with Jersey at her side. He watched as Carson's truck stopped in the driveway.

"I have to walk her out," Rebecca said. She put his tea in front of him and then she was gone.

Isaac leaned over the cup, holding it tight with both hands. After a few minutes he took a cautious sip. And another. His head pounded and if he moved too quickly, the world spun for a few seconds.

The back door banged shut and footsteps heralded Rebecca's return to the kitchen. He took another sip of the tea and prayed the awkward moment would be ignored and she wouldn't feel like talking about what her daughter had said. The last thing he wanted to do right now was talk emotions.

"I'm sorry," she said, as she entered the kitchen. "She just…"

He held up a hand to stop her. "She's a little girl who wants a dad. I'm no poster child for fatherhood, but I'm here. End of story."

"That isn't true," she argued.

"Isn't it?"

She rummaged in a drawer, bottom lip between her teeth, and he wondered if she was trying not to cry. He wasn't going to ask, because if he was avoiding emotion, that would be the worst thing to do. Instead he drank his tea as she went from drawer to drawer.

"Can I help you find something?" he asked.

She shook her head. She had a towel in her hand, a small vial of lavender and a clear plastic baggie. He watched as she filled the bag with ice, got the towel damp, added drops of the oil and then wrapped it around the bag.

The stove timer went off. She tossed the towel concoction on the counter and removed the cinnamon rolls. His appetite suddenly perked up.

He wouldn't mind a cup of coffee and a cinnamon roll.

Rebecca picked up the towel and moved around behind him.

"Lean forward," she ordered.

He glanced back at her. "Do what?"

"Cross your arms and lean forward on them. I don't know if this will help but it's worth a try."

He did what she'd asked and she placed the cold towel across the back of his neck. The scent of lavender floated around him. He'd always considered himself a manly guy, but he didn't mind a little bit of pampering from time to time. This felt a lot like being pampered.

As he rested his head, she stood behind him, making him a little nervous. Then her fingers settled on his ears and she began to massage.

"Something I learned from a friend," she told him.

"I'm glad." He closed his eyes as her hands moved to his temples and circled lightly.

"What brought the headache on?"

"Nightmare," he admitted. He hadn't planned on telling her, but the tea and the lavender had relaxed him. "I punched Joe when he tried to wake me."

She laughed a little. "I'm sorry, that isn't funny. But I can imagine his surprise."

"Yeah." Isaac drew in a deep breath as she moved her hands to his shoulders. "Where have you been all my life?"

"Stop it," she whispered.

She was right.

"I don't think you should go to the shop alone."

Her hands stilled and then they were gone. "I have to go. I can't let him control what I do or don't do. If I'm going to live here, I have to open the salon. If I'm not going to open it, I might as well admit I'm a coward and leave town."

"You're not a coward." He sat back up, the headache now the faintest throb. "You're a woman who's determined to succeed. I get that. But you can't put your life in jeopardy. Let's give the police a few days to find him."

"We have no way of knowing where he's hiding. I can't put off opening the place. I signed a contract with Jack to start a business. That means I have to open it."

"Jack understands what's going on, that your life is in danger."

Rebecca had moved around the island from him. She placed two cinnamon rolls on plates and slid one in front of him.

"You really should eat something." She met his gaze, unwavering and strong. Her warm chocolate eyes drew him in, holding him captive.

"Rebecca," he started.

She shook her head. "I have to go. I have to make this work."

"I understand. We all have to fight our battles the best way we know how."

At that moment he was battling what was a definite attraction to the woman standing across from him.

It was a battle he was losing

He'd been sitting in front of her salon for an hour. She'd seen him pull up and thought he might come in.

She'd been ready for him, planning exactly what she'd say should he walk through the door.

She'd also managed to give Mattie, the former owner of Mattie's Café, a perm. She wanted to look nice at the Christmas parade on Saturday. Yes, it would be dark, but a woman couldn't just neglect her appearance. Not even a woman in her seventh decade, Mattie had informed Rebecca.

She chatted with Mattie about the church Christmas program, how pretty the lights around town looked and the way Jack had decorated Lakeside Resort. She dodged any questions about her family. Grove was a good thirty miles away. That didn't mean that people didn't know the Barneses.

"Now I know you're not listening," Mattie said. At the same time she glanced in the mirror and turned her head first right and then left. Her gray curls were cut just above her shoulders and she patted them and smiled. "You aren't listening, but you did a mighty fine job with these old curls of mine. I look like that actress. I can't remember her name, but she has gray, curly hair."

"You look beautiful, Mattie," Rebecca told the woman. She handed her a mirror so she could examine the back.

"Well, I think you're going to be a welcome addition to this town. Since Janice Tucker retired, we've had to drive twenty minutes to get our hair done or do it ourselves. And you saw the result of that."

Mattie's hair had been a little uneven.

"It wasn't bad," she told the older woman.

"Now that isn't quite true." Mattie looked toward the front of the shop. "Is that why you're distracted?"

"I'm sorry?"

Mattie handed her back the mirror. "Isaac West has been sitting out there in his truck. He has his hat pulled down and appears to be asleep. But every now and then he looks this way. And every now and then you sigh. He's a lot like his daddy. Or a lot like Jack is now and the way Jack could have been if he hadn't spent twenty-some years of his life living in the bottle and fighting mad. The problem with Isaac is he thinks he's a carbon copy of Jack. Full stop."

"They are alike." Rebecca hoped she could say that much and not get dragged further into the conversation.

But Mattie liked to talk. "Oh, he's as good-looking as his daddy. All three of those boys look like Jack. They couldn't deny him and he can't deny them. His daughter, Daisy, also looks like Jack, but prettier."

"Mmm-hmm," Rebecca mumbled, reaching for her hair spray. "I'm going to give this a touch of spray. Close your eyes."

Mattie did, but kept on talking. "I thought he'd get married to the Davis girl. He dated her in high school."

"Umm-hmm." Rebecca applied the light mist.

"He had a flashback, right out in front of the café. Someone said it had to do with fireworks. Or one of those things teenagers like to set off that you can hear in three counties."

"He was in Vietnam, wasn't he?" Rebecca asked.

Mattie opened her eyes. Their gazes met in the reflection of the mirror. "Oh, honey, I wasn't talking about Jack. I was talking about Isaac. He loved that girl. But he broke things off with her. When he heard that explosion, he pushed her to the ground, trying to keep her safe. Jack said he doubts Isaac will ever let another woman in his life. He was that upset he'd hurt the Davis girl. Ruth was her name. Good girl. Ended up married to a doctor in Tulsa." Mattie grabbed her purse and pulled out several twenties. "You keep the change."

And then she hugged Rebecca and was gone.

Rebecca walked to the front of the salon, glad for the break. She knew people were being kind, but it was noon and she'd been busy since she opened at nine. She studied the man in the truck and knew he was watching her, even though his head was down and his hat pulled low.

For a moment she thought about going out there and telling him to go home. But then she thought about how noble it was, that he'd been sitting out there all this time. Keeping her safe. She picked up her phone and called Mattie's Café. Holly answered.

"Holly, I'd like to place an order and I wondered if it could be delivered."

"Well, of course. I've noticed you've been busy over there. I hope you're able to take an afternoon customer. I think I'll have a break around two."

"Holly, your hair is beautiful. You don't need to have a thing done and we both know that."

"Dead ends, honey. You know how that keeps a girl's hair from growing."

Rebecca shook her head, even though Holly couldn't see.

"What is it you want delivered?" Holly asked.

"It isn't for me," she admitted. "See the stubborn cowboy in the truck, sitting in front of my salon and scaring off well-meaning citizens?"

"The overprotective one with the black cowboy hat?"

"That's the one. Could you deliver him his favorite lunch, and I'll pay you for it?"

Holly laughed for a good minute. "You bet I will. Honey, you sure are making this town more interesting."

"I'm trying."

"And what about you? Your favorite chef salad?" Holly asked.

"Yes, thanks, that would be good."

The call ended. Isaac shifted a bit and she knew he was watching. She blew him a kiss and walked off, smiling all the while.

Not fifteen minutes later, as she was tidying her work area, the door opened. When she turned to look, she stopped sweeping because it wasn't Holly stopping in to get paid for the delivery. Isaac lifted a bag that held take-out containers.

"Did you order me lunch?" he asked.

"Someone has to take care of you," she told him. She opened the utility closet and placed the broom on the hook. "You know you don't have to stand guard."

"I kind of feel as if I do. For Allie's sake. She needs you."

Rebecca thought of the woman he'd dated, the one everyone had thought he might marry. She wondered if it had broken his heart when he broke things off with her. It probably had. He was that kind of man, the kind who pretended he was tough as nails and could handle anything—which he likely could. But he also probably loved with the same loyalty that he gave to his friends.

She felt a stirring of envy that she quickly tamped down.

"Rebecca?"

The question drew her back to the present. He stood there studying her as if he hadn't quite figured out what to do with her.

"I'm sorry. Lost in thought."

"I brought our lunch. Thank you for ordering."

"You're welcome. And thank you for watching out for me. I do appreciate it. I just know that you have better things to do with your time."

"Better things than sitting outside your salon watching you work? I don't think so."

"That's a little creepy," she teased.

"I'm just saying, it wasn't just a bad deal for me."

She walked away from him. "I don't want you to feel as if you're responsible for me. I know we live on the ranch and Mercy Ranch is a family. I just… This morning, what Allie said…"

"I know."

He knew. She wished this could have been simple. She wished they had met, gone their separate ways, seeing each other from time to time as they passed at the café or even at church.

Instead, they were tangled up in one another's lives, and Allie was the other thread, the most important and fragile thread.

Fortunately, the chime over the door announced another customer, and Rebecca left him sitting with his club sandwich while she tended to his aunt Lola's hair.

But as she leaned his aunt back to wash her hair, her attention slid to the cowboy sitting across the room, his jean-clad legs stretched out in front of him. He was watching her and his expression held her for a moment.

What would happen if their lives became so intertwined, connecting them in a way that they'd never unravel?

Chapter Twelve

Saturday arrived and it was the best weather day they'd had in a week. The sun was shining and the temperature soared to a balmy, mid-December sixty degrees. Even at five o'clock as they were gathering at the school where the parade would begin, the temperature was still close to fifty.

Isaac unloaded his horse, Buster, and tied him to the side of the trailer. He went back in for the extra horses for others from the ranch who wanted to ride, Sierra, Joe and a few of the other men. Jack stood nearby. He wouldn't ride, but he'd be watching from the sidelines.

A second trailer backed in next to Isaac's. Carson got out of his truck and waved, but went right to work unloading horses for himself and Kylie. Andy and Maggie would ride double with their parents. Isaac finished with his own livestock and stepped over to see if he could help his brother.

"Need any assistance?"

Carson pointed to his daughter. "Corral Maggie before she takes off on my horse and we have to call the law to run her down."

Isaac grinned at his niece, who had blond curls and big blue eyes. She was trouble. The worst kind. "Maggie, are you causing problems?"

She giggled and shook her head. "No, I just want a pony."

"There you have it. Uncle Isaac will have to take care of that for you. But since you're in trouble, why don't you help me? I need to check on Allie. She's going to be on the church float."

Maggie wasn't really paying attention to him. He didn't blame her. There was a lot going on. More and more floats were arriving. Local fire trucks and police officers were lining up for the parade. People were everywhere. And it signaled danger to Isaac.

Greg had been quiet for the past week, lying low. That didn't mean he was gone. Isaac scanned the area, looking for the man Rebecca had described to him and to the police. He walked past a float decorated with a miniature church and a group of people dressed as carolers.

The next float was from another local church. They'd somehow created what looked to be a snow globe around the baby Jesus.

The Community Church float was at the back of the line, holding a living nativity scene complete with people, animals, the stable. And angels. Allie happened to be one of the angels.

Still no sign of Greg.

"There's Allie." Maggie pointed. "She looks pretty."

"Look at that costume," Isaac said.

"She lights up." Maggie tried to hurry off. He had hold of her hand and stopped her.

"Nope, you have to stay with me. We'll walk over together and check on her."

Maggie sighed. "Okay. And then we get to ride our horses?"

"And then we get to ride."

"Does your horse have lights?"

He winked at his niece. "That's a surprise. You'll find out."

"I bet you do."

"You're mighty impatient."

She pulled him toward the float. Allie saw them and waved. Her face was lit up. Next to her, Jersey, overcome by the excitement, barked. Rebecca stood at the side of the float, her face serious. She was probably giving her daughter last-minute instructions.

Isaac stepped up to her. "She'll be fine," he said.

"Of course she will." Rebecca motioned her daughter close. "Give me a hug."

"Oh, Mom."

"I can't help it. I'm a mom. It's what we do. We give instructions. We worry."

Someone called out that the parade was about to start and everyone needed to get in place. Isaac could hear bands practicing. A band or two would march between the floats, and then before the horses. No one wanted to follow the horses.

"We have to go." He reached for Maggie's hand, but looked at Rebecca. She'd been working all week, trying to start the salon right and preparing for her open house. He'd kept an eye on her, but he knew that local police had also been patrolling by on a regular basis.

Maggie pulled on his hand. He looked up and saw his brother not twenty feet away. He let go of his niece's hand and she ran to her father, jumping as he lifted her into his arms. Carson was a good dad. He'd been a single dad, having lost his wife in a car accident. She'd been pregnant with Maggie when the accident occurred and had only lived long enough for her baby to be delivered.

"She's fine," Isaac told Rebecca, speaking of Allie. "I won't be more than a hundred feet behind her. And there are plenty of people on the float who will be watching her."

"I'm not worried about a seizure," she told Isaac. "I'm worried about Greg. He hasn't left town. He doesn't give up that easily. I know he's watching, waiting for the right time."

"I'll watch for him. You can't live your life in fear. Allie needs to be a kid and do what other kids do."

"I know that," she said. Her expression softened. "I've missed…"

He waited, but she wouldn't say it. Smart woman. Instead she shifted, glancing back at the float where her daughter stood ready to be an angel, heralding one of history's most important events.

"I should go," he told Rebecca. "Enjoy the parade."

She stood on tiptoe and kissed his cheek. "Thank you for being my friend."

"You're welcome." He watched her walk away and then hurried to mount Buster. Friends. Even the word was uncomplicated. No ties. No worries about the future. Nice, uncomplicated friendship.

He'd given up on complicated. The day he'd shoved Ruth Davis to the ground, he'd realized that his new life didn't need to include a woman.

He needed his life to be uncomplicated. The fewer

people he had to worry about, the better. But the little girl on the float ahead of him... He couldn't pretend he didn't care about her life, about keeping her safe. Or her mother.

The parade rolled slowly away from the school. Fire trucks and police cars went first. At random intervals their sirens cut through the quiet night. The exception was the old fire truck with the Christmas lights. A Christmas carol played from the speaker on the hood. The passengers tossed handfuls of candy and children hurried to grab up what they could.

This was the best part of small town life. He'd once been a little boy standing on the sidewalk as the parade rolled down the street. His mom had never joined him. But he would walk to town and watch the parade by himself. Of course, he'd act as if he didn't want that candy, but after everyone was gone, he'd grab up the leftovers.

The bands were staggered, so they didn't all go through at once, competing with different carols. The floats from local churches and businesses were staged between the bands.

Intermittently, he would catch part of a song one of the bands played. He heard bits and pieces of "Silent Night," "Joy to the World" and "Little Town of Bethlehem" as area schools did their best to bring Christmas cheer to the small community.

They were nearly back to the school when he saw the man come out of the crowd and approach Allie's float. He hurried alongside it, yelling something that Isaac couldn't hear, but it was clear as day he was yelling at Allie. Isaac nudged Buster forward, but Greg shot a look in his direction and then took off through the crowds, disappearing into the night.

Isaac rode up to the float. Allie's face matched the pale ivory of her angel costume and she was visibly trembling. One of the adults on the float hugged her, but Isaac knew no one but her own mother would do at the moment. He wrapped the reins around the saddle horn and held his arms out to her.

"Come on. I won't let you fall." Buster did a nervous jig, but with a soft word from Isaac, the horse settled.

For a full minute the little girl hesitated. She moved to the edge of the float and looked from him to the crowd beyond. Her eyes were stark with fear as she fell into his arms. She was tiny, but her entire body trembled, and she clung to him with all her nine-year-old might.

"Who was that man?" she asked.

"Don't worry about it. We'll catch him." What else should he say?

"He wasn't nice."

"No, he isn't nice, but he won't bother you again." He shifted her so that he could hold her tight while still keeping control of Buster. "What did he say to you, Allie?"

"He's my daddy, isn't he, Isaac?"

"Let's find your mom, Al."

"But Jersey…" She peeked back over his shoulder. "She's still on the float. Oh. She jumped."

"Crazy dog."

A sharp bark demanded that he wait. He pulled up on Buster's reins, and sure enough, Jersey was heading their way. She wasn't about to let Allie be on her own. Isaac doubted she would have let Greg anywhere near the girl.

But it wasn't physical harm Isaac was concerned about. A man like Greg could do a lot of harm with words.

As they rode back up to the school, Rebecca came running. She had a look of terror in her eyes, but when she saw Allie safe in his arms she stopped, took a deep breath and managed to appear calm.

Isaac eased the child to the ground and she immediately ran into Rebecca's arms. Words tumbled out, about the man. Her father.

"You said he wasn't a nice man. He isn't nice, Mom. He isn't nice at all." Allie continued to hold Rebecca tight.

As the parade meandered past them, Isaac swung his leg over Buster's back and dismounted, nearly tripping over Jersey as he did so. The dog moved quickly, but gave Isaac a condescending look, if that was possible for a canine.

"I'm going to find a deputy." Isaac led Buster through the crowd, needing to do something proactive to help Rebecca and Allie. Something that didn't include pulling the two of them close and telling them he would never let anyone hurt them.

Rebecca led her daughter through the crowds, unsure where to go. She spotted Isaac's truck and trailer and headed in that direction, as if Isaac were her true north. But he wasn't, she reminded herself. He was a cowboy who could be charming, caring and emotionally closed off.

"Why is he here?" Allie asked. The question set off

warning bells. Rebecca glanced around, looking for Greg. He was nowhere to be seen.

"He's gone now," she assured her daughter.

"No, why is he here? In Hope."

"I guess he thought he should be able to meet you. I'm sorry, Allie. I never wanted to hurt you or have him hurt you this way. He isn't a good person. He's been in prison. That's why you've never met him before now."

Red lights flashed through the night. Allie glanced toward the line of emergency vehicles. The lights dimmed as the parade ended. The parade had been beautiful. A perfect example of cheerful, small-town life. One of the traditions that continued even as the world changed, moved a little faster.

Greg shouldn't be able to ruin it for them.

Jersey moved closer to Allie, nuzzling her arm and whining. Allie reached for the dog, then her eyes changed, the way they always did right before a seizure. Rebecca spoke her name but Allie didn't respond. Her body started to tremble. Rebecca reached to lower her to the ground. Allie sagged in her arms and sweet Jersey stayed glued to her side as she began to convulse on the cold pavement.

Rebecca dropped to her knees, praying. Really praying for the first time in a long time. Because she couldn't do this on her own. She was so tired of being alone. She was tired of not having her parents to call when things like this happened. She'd had no one for so long.

Just then a hand settled on her shoulder and squeezed— Isaac, letting her know he was there.

"Carson," he yelled, getting his brother's attention.

And then he dropped to his knees next to her and began to pray for Allie, as if she was precious to him.

Rebecca blinked away tears that clouded her vision.

"She's going to be okay," Isaac assured her.

Carson appeared and Jack was with him. "How long?" Carson asked.

Rebecca glanced at her watch. Three minutes. Allie's body stilled. She remained motionless.

"Allie, wake up, honey." Rebecca leaned close, using a tissue to wipe her daughter's face. She placed a palm on her cheek, stroking it the way she always did. The way she'd been doing since her daughter was a tiny infant. Long before the seizures.

This was when she always woke up. She had to wake up.

Her eyes fluttered. "Mommy," she cried.

And then her eyes rolled back and another seizure gripped her tiny body.

"We're going to the hospital, Rebecca." Carson spoke as the physician now.

Isaac stood. "I'll get the ambulance."

Carson nodded and took his place next to Allie. "Take a deep breath, Rebecca."

She tried. She really tried. But the tears wouldn't stop. She couldn't make them. "I'm so afraid for her."

"I know, but she's going to be fine. We'll get her on the ambulance and I'll be able to help her more than I can right now."

"Can I ride with her?" Rebecca leaned over her daughter, smoothing her hair as the seizure finally ended.

"That one was shorter," Carson assured her. "And I'd

rather you not ride in the ambulance. It's crowded and I'm going to be in there. Let Isaac drive you to Grove."

She nodded, accepting but not wanting to be separated from Allie. She understood, though the idea of not being with her was torture.

The ambulance crew headed their way with medical equipment and a gurney. Carson was on his feet directing them. He lifted Allie gently and placed her on the gurney, strapping her in so that she wouldn't fall.

Rebecca walked next to her daughter, promising her she'd be at the hospital waiting for her. Allie's eyes were open and she nodded, barely. Jersey ran alongside the gurney, and before they could stop her, she jumped into the ambulance.

"Let her go," Rebecca said. "Please, Carson, let her take the dog."

Strong arms wrapped around Rebecca and she was pulled back against a firm chest. Isaac. Still there with her. She wasn't alone.

"Be calm. The dog goes." His words were murmured close to her ear.

Carson glanced back at his brother and nodded. "The dog goes."

Rebecca refused to move away from the ambulance. Until the doors closed and the lights came on, she stood watching as they worked on her daughter, a tiny form in the back of the vehicle, so tiny. Her heart quaked with fear, with sadness.

Strong arms continued to hold her. Isaac told her to trust, to have faith. As the ambulance rolled away, she turned into his embrace and he hugged her tight.

"Let's go," he finally said.

They turned and Jack was there standing behind

them. She'd forgotten Jack. He glanced at his son, questions in his eyes, and then he gave Rebecca a quick hug.

"She's going to be okay. You've got the best doctor in the state. Top trauma surgeon back in Texas." Jack smiled and awkwardly patted her shoulder. "You two go on to the hospital. Maria is here—she'll drive me home. I don't want you to think you have to worry about me."

"Thank you, Jack." Rebecca kissed his cheek. "You mean a lot to Allie and me."

"You're part of our family now." He glanced toward the road as the ambulance siren sounded through the evening. "Now you two go on. I'm going to talk to the police and see if they've spotted that yahoo. I'll call if I learn anything."

"Thanks, Jack." Isaac took her by the hand and led her to his truck. The same truck she'd been heading for just fifteen minutes earlier. Had it been only fifteen minutes? It seemed like forever.

Isaac opened the truck door and she climbed in. He stood there for a moment with the door open. "I'm sorry."

"It isn't your fault."

"No, but I wish I could have stopped him. If I'd gotten to him sooner…"

"Yes, well, I wish I had realized sooner what kind of person he is." She sighed.

He closed the door and appeared a moment later on the driver's side. He climbed behind the wheel and fired up the diesel engine of the truck.

"I should call my parents," she said as she looked out the side window. "I want to call them. Isn't that silly? They've wanted nothing to do with us all this time. My father has said horrible things to me, about my daughter, and yet I want him to be at the hospital. I want to know that I have family. Someone out there has to care about us."

"People care." He spoke the words simply. Then he glanced her way. And she saw in his eyes that he did care. The realization warmed her and yet, it troubled her, too. Wanting him to care, needing him to care, felt like emotional quicksand.

"I know." She let the words out, not seeking answers from him that she knew would complicate things more.

"Do you? Do you realize how many people care? Jack, Carson and Kylie, me. Half the town is already in love with you and Allie."

"And here I am wishing for more." Not fishing for more, she wanted to tell him.

"No, that isn't what I meant to imply. I just want you to know that, no matter what your parents do or don't do, you're not alone. But I don't blame you for wanting them. Call them."

"What if they tell me they don't care? What if my dad says something like it's my fault?"

"Then I'm here for you. And honestly, I might have to take him before the church and point out his sins."

Laughter bubbled up and it shook loose some of the fear that had encased her heart. She pulled her phone out of her purse and dialed the number. After a few rings, it was answered.

Rebecca suddenly found it hard to breathe. She closed her eyes and forced air into her lungs.

"Mom." She started to cry. She hadn't wanted to, but she couldn't control the tears. She couldn't pretend it was just a few drops, either; torrents of tears fell down her cheeks. A warm hand reached for hers, holding tight.

"Mom, Allie…" she sobbed, and the words wouldn't come.

"Honey, is she okay? Rebecca, take a deep breath and talk to me."

"Mom, she's on her way to the hospital in Grove. She's having seizures. I'm so afraid for her."

"We'll be there." No hesitation. No condemnation. They would be there.

"Please…" Rebecca begged, and she knew she didn't have to. Her mother had already said she would be there.

"Rebecca, of course. Now, you're not driving yourself, are you?"

She shook her head. "No."

"Okay, we'll see you there."

She nodded and clicked off. Isaac's hand still held hers. He wasn't letting go. But he would. Eventually. She knew that he was there for her, but that he wouldn't let himself be more than a friend.

For that moment a friend was exactly what she needed. But she worried that if he stayed too long in her life, she might want him to stay forever.

Chapter Thirteen

Rebecca entered the hospital with Isaac at her side. The emergency room of the small hospital wasn't crowded. She scanned the few people in the waiting room. Then her vision tunneled and for a minute everything went fuzzy as her father stood up. Tall with thinning dark hair, glasses perched on his nose and his customary suit... She remembered the last time she'd seen him. She'd always hated that suit. Always hated the way he'd studied her over the top of his glasses.

Today she felt a mixture of emotions. Anger, hurt, relief. He put the magazine he held back on the table next to him and took a few steps in her direction. She was torn. She needed to check on Allie. But she needed to thank her parents for being there.

"Rebecca." He said it with his same firm voice. She remembered being a little girl sitting on his lap as he read to her, and he'd always had that voice. A preacher's voice, she thought. As if God had known his calling and had given him the voice to match.

"Dad."

He cleared his throat, clearly uncomfortable. Maybe he'd thought he could be here and not actually see them.

"Your mother went to find a vending machine. She needed water."

Some things never changed. Her mother always went in search of a vending machine and a bottle of water. Rebecca guessed it might be a nervous habit.

Doors behind them opened. Carson approached and he looked calm. As if everything would be okay. That was a good sign, wasn't it?

"She's okay. She had one more seizure. We've stopped them. She's awake and wants her mom. And Jersey is having a difficult time allowing hospital staff near the bed. So you might want to do something with your dog, Isaac."

"I can take her home."

A moment of panic hit Rebecca. "You can't leave."

"Okay, I won't leave."

"I'm sorry." She rubbed her hands down her arms. "You can go. I know you have things to do."

"I'm not leaving. Not right now. When I do go home, I'll take Jersey. And I'll get her now and take her for a walk. I'm sure you're wanting to see Allie."

"I can take you back there." Carson gave Rebecca's father a curious look.

She had to explain. "Dr. West, this is my father, Pastor Don Barnes."

"I see. Mr. Barnes, it's good to meet you."

"Thank you, Dr. West. And my wife, Alice, is here, as well." He looked back over his shoulder. "She's off searching for a vending machine."

"Well, if you'd like to come with Rebecca..."

He shook his head. "No, I think I'll wait."

The hesitance in his voice didn't surprise Rebecca. He'd spent nine years pretending he didn't have a granddaughter. One night wouldn't change that.

"You go. I'll see her soon." Don Barnes took a step back and Rebecca let him. Because prayers could be answered, but it wasn't a night for miracles. He was there. She could accept that as a place to begin.

The door near the back of the waiting room opened and her mother hurried in, carrying a bottle of water and a candy bar. She saw them, rushed forward and hugged Rebecca tightly.

"How is Allie?" she asked breathlessly.

"She's better. Dr. West was giving us an update. I'm going back to see her if you'd like to come?"

Unlike her father, Rebecca's mom didn't hesitate. "Of course I want to see her." She held up the chocolate. "I bought her a candy bar."

Rebecca looked to Carson and he nodded. "She can have it."

Isaac still stood there. "You should come, too," Rebecca said.

Carson led the three of them through the door to the emergency room. "I'm going to have her stay the night, just to make sure she's past this. Tomorrow we'll run some tests."

He pulled back a curtain and motioned them inside the cubicle. Allie looked small and fragile in the hospital bed. Her dark eyes seemed darker in her pale face. She was wrapped in a thin hospital blanket, her attention focused on the TV that hung from the wall. When they entered, she sat up, her glittery angel wings fluttering behind her, creased and smudged with dirt.

"Mommy," she cried out. She rarely called Rebecca

that anymore. For the last couple of years it had been "Mom." After all, she would be ten in the fall.

Rebecca hugged her, crumpling the wings further.

"We should take these off," Rebecca said as she reached to unclasp the wings. "You're okay, you know. Everything is going to be just fine."

"I hope I never see that man again," Allie stated with a healthy dose of anger. "He said to tell you he's going to get the money out of you…"

She put a finger to Allie's lips. "Shh, don't worry about him."

Allie looked past her, her head cocking to the side and her eyes narrowing. She leaned close. "Who is that?"

Rebecca whispered in her ear, "That's your grandmother."

"Your mom," Allie whispered back.

Rebecca smiled and pulled her daughter close. "Yes. Oh, Allie, I love you so much."

"I love you, too." And then she raised her head to peek over the other shoulder. "And Isaac. He rescued me."

"Yes, he did. We should thank him, too."

Allie grinned. "Thank you, Isaac."

"You're welcome. I'm going to take Jersey for a walk. But, Allie, if you need anything, you ring that buzzer of yours and tell them to come find me."

She nodded. "I will, Isaac."

He left with her dog, and Rebecca reached out to pull her mother close. "Mom, this is Allie. Your granddaughter."

Her mother began to sob. "Oh, Allie, you are just as beautiful as your mom. I have missed knowing you."

Rebecca could tell her daughter didn't quite know what to say. Fortunately a nurse entered the room with a hospital gown for the young patient. And right after she'd changed Carson reappeared to tell them they would be going to a hospital room soon.

Allie shook her head at the announcement. "I want to go home."

Carson pulled a stool close to the bed. "And you will go home. Tomorrow. Tonight you're going to stay so we can keep an eye on you. Your mom can stay, too. We'll put you in a room with two beds, one for each of you. And if your grandmother wants to stay, we can bring in a chair bed."

"Like a slumber party?" Allie asked.

A nurse slipped into the room. "Exactly like a slumber party. We even have a DVD player and you can watch movies. And if you're hungry, we'll have pizza delivered."

"You can do that?" Allie asked.

Carson laughed. "I've learned that these nurses can make just about anything happen."

Allie leaned back on the pillow. "Okay, I'll stay."

He patted her shoulder. "Thanks for agreeing. Okay, Nurse Jenkins, let's take our patient to her room."

Allie sat back up. "Where's Isaac and Jersey?"

"I'm not certain, but I'll go find them," Carson assured her. "I'll see that he says goodbye before he leaves."

"Does he have to leave?" Allie looked from Carson to her mother and back again.

"He doesn't have to," Carson answered. "But he's not the best at sleeping in a chair. He gets cranky."

And he has nightmares. Rebecca knew that he

wouldn't want to sleep in public, where others might be witness to one of his dreams or, worse, get too close when he woke up from one.

He was an expert at not allowing people to get too close. Even though it appeared he'd been dragged, possibly against his will, into their lives.

Jersey led him all around the outside of the hospital. Isaac pretended it was about taking the dog for a walk, but he needed time to get his thoughts and emotions under control. He also needed to know that Greg wasn't lurking anywhere near the facility.

Finally, he went back inside. The cold air had helped clear his mind.

Or so he'd thought. As he walked through the emergency waiting room, he spotted Don Barnes, Rebecca's father. He approached the man, unsure what he should say. Yeah, he could think of a lot of things he wanted to tell the other man, but that was different from what he *should* say.

"Have they updated you about Allie?" he asked, as he took a seat across from Mr. Barnes. He pointed and Jersey sat.

"They're moving her to a room and keeping her overnight."

"I'm sure you're relieved," Isaac said.

"Yes, I am. If I may ask, exactly how do you know my daughter and granddaughter?"

"They're living at Mercy Ranch right now, owned by my father, Jack West."

"I see. Are you and Rebecca dating?"

"No, we're just friends. She has a lot of friends in Hope. She's actually gone back to church."

Pastor Barnes took off his glasses and started cleaning them. "I'm a pastor, Mr. West, a Christian, a man of God. I'm not perfect. My only child made mistakes that I never thought she'd make."

"God's children let Him down every single day."

"Yes, we do. I can't undo the past, Mr. West. I can't force my daughter to forgive me. I can only do my best going forward."

Again Isaac had to bite his tongue. He didn't have a horse in this show, so he might as well back off and let this family fix their own mess. He just didn't want Allie to be the one hurt.

"I'll leave you in peace." Isaac stood.

Rebecca's father stopped him. "I'm glad she has good friends."

Isaac walked away, Jersey at his side. He didn't have a plan. Maybe he'd find the cafeteria. Or a vending machine. After that he'd find Allie's room and reunite her with Jersey. It had been years since he'd been to this hospital. The last time, he'd been twelve and had a broken arm after getting tossed off a green broke horse.

If he remembered correctly, he had to make a right and then a left to get to the cafeteria. As he made the first right, he noticed a gift shop. The door was open and the lights were on.

He entered and a lady at the counter glanced up. "We're not open."

"Oh, I'm sorry." He started to leave.

"Nice dog."

"Thank you. She's a service animal. Her owner is a patient in the hospital."

The lady came around the counter. "Can I pet her?"

"Of course. Her name is Jersey."

"That's...unique."

He laughed. "It's the eyes. She has the eyes of a Jersey cow."

"Well, I guess she might. Was there something specific you were looking for?"

He thought for a moment, then gave the easy answer. "Yeah, something for a little girl."

"Her owner?"

"Yes."

"Stuffed animals, children's books, drawing paper and colored pencils. Take your pick." She gestured to a corner of the store.

He thanked her and headed in the direction of the children's gifts. On the way he spotted jewelry. A pretty bracelet caught his attention. It was the type that women liked, with beads and charms she could add. He studied the charms and found a dog, scissors, a cowboy hat. Too much. He put the hat back.

Footsteps behind him warned that he wasn't alone. He turned and saw Carson grinning at him.

"That is a mistake unless you want to make a statement."

Isaac dropped the charms back in the tray. "What's that supposed to mean?"

"If you're buying that bracelet for Allie, that's a nice thing to do. But she might prefer a stuffed animal. If you're buying that bracelet for her mother, you'd better mean it."

"Mean what?"

"Jewelry, Isaac. Do I have to spell it out to you? I know you're a bachelor for life and all that nonsense, but you do date. Don't you?"

"Seldom. Why date if you're not interested in marriage? That just leads to complications. A date means 'I think I might like to get to know you better.' And don't you look at me like I'm a foreign species."

"No, I think that's admirable. Why lead someone on if you're not interested in a relationship? But you're looking at jewelry."

Isaac scrubbed a hand over his face and groaned. "Oh, man, I'm not sure what's gotten into me."

His brother hit him on the back, hard. "Yeah, I think I might know. And if you're not interested, even though you are, don't buy the jewelry."

"You're right." He spotted a pretty pink diary and a set of colored pens. "I see something Allie would like."

"I'm going to head home, now that we've got her settled. Are you going home soon? If so, I could use a ride. Kylie is at home and Maggie's asleep."

"Yeah, sure, just let me pay for this and I'll take you home."

He paid, thanking the woman at the register. As he walked with Carson in the direction of Allie's room, he changed his mind.

"You know what? I'm not going home."

"What? Why?"

"I can't leave them here alone," he explained. "What if Greg realizes she's here?"

"They have security," Carson pointed out.

"Yeah, one guy with keys that rattle. I saw him. If he's not right outside their room, he can't do a thing." But maybe he wasn't needed? "Is Mrs. Barnes staying?"

"Rebecca's parents left a few minutes ago. Isaac, I don't think he is showing up here tonight."

He pulled his keys out of his pocket and handed them

to his brother. Carson took them, looked at the keys, then at Isaac. "You don't like to sleep near other people."

"So I won't sleep. I'll stay awake."

Rebecca stepped out of Allie's room. "You have to sleep. Go home, Isaac. We'll be fine."

She'd been listening. Great. "I'm staying."

"Because you think you need to." She came closer and it was all he could do not to draw her into his arms and tell her he wouldn't let anyone hurt her. Including himself. Which was why he shoved his hands in his pockets and backed up.

"I'm staying because I want to stay. I love sleeping in hospital waiting rooms. Only a coldhearted woman would deny me the opportunity."

"As far as arguments go, that one was top-notch. I'm almost convinced." Carson shook his head. "Let him stay. He'll be here if you need anything."

Rebecca eyed him. Then finally relented. "Okay then, stay."

"Thank you. And if you don't mind, I have something for Allie."

She stepped to the side, giving him space to enter the room. He dropped Jersey's harness. The dog immediately went to her mistress, standing on hind legs and placing her front paws and head on the bed next to Allie.

"Jersey!" Allie leaned to hug her. "I missed you."

"No dogs allowed in the hospital." The nurse who entered the room gave Isaac a look that pinned him as the guilty one.

"Jersey is your patient's service dog."

"Oh, I see. Well, then I guess we can make an exception for dogs named after cows. At least she isn't a cow. I would have to draw the line at cows in the room."

The nurse winked at Allie, then continued, "What I do have is a DVD player, several movies and pizza that's going to be delivered soon."

"Pizza?" Isaac glanced back at his brother.

"Pizza is fine." Carson leaned against the wall and watched his patient, her mother, and then Isaac.

"I don't remember ever having pizza in a hospital."

"Things change." Carson glanced at his watch. "I'm going to head home, but I'll be back in the morning. Allie, you are to relax and rest. I know you're probably groggy and that's normal. Don't stay up and party too late."

She laughed at the warning. "Okay, Dr. West."

On his way out the door Carson gave Isaac another one of those deadly pats on the back, the kind that made a guy almost fall over. "Stay out of trouble, bro."

"Thanks for the warning."

Isaac moved farther into the room, closer to the bed, closer to Rebecca. It did him good to see Allie, to know she was definitely on the mend. Her eyes were bright and her skin had lost that pasty white-as-grandma's-sheets look.

"Do you want pizza?" Rebecca offered. "You have to eat."

"I'm good. I'll get something from the vending machine."

"Nonsense," she said. "Stay and eat."

He would stay. But he knew he was walking on dangerous ground. The kind that could swallow him up at any second. She could do that to him. It had to do with her smile. Or maybe the way she leaned into him as if she didn't even realize she was doing it.

Whatever the case, she was his kryptonite.

Chapter Fourteen

Isaac had been in and out of Allie's room all night. Each time Rebecca had woken up, she'd noticed him at the door, watching. Jersey had seemed just as vigilant. At eight in the morning, though, Isaac seemed to have gone missing. She hadn't seen him in several hours. She guessed he'd probably fallen asleep in the waiting room.

"Why don't you go find him?" Her mother's simple question took Rebecca by surprise. Alice Barnes had showed up shortly before breakfast was served.

"I'm sorry?"

"Your friend, the one who pulled the all-night security detail outside the room. The nurses told me when I got here. They dragged a chair over for him to use." Alice smiled. "I guessed he might be the reason you keep looking at the clock and then at the door."

"No, I'm just wondering when we get to leave."

"I'm sure you are. And you're wondering where he's gone off to. He's very nice."

"He's just a friend." She stood up, stretching to relieve the kinks in her spine. "I think I will go check on him."

She kissed Allie on the forehead and left the room. The most obvious waiting room was empty. As was the emergency waiting room. She remembered her father sitting there the previous evening, the worried look on his face. Before they'd gone home, he'd come to Allie's room for a brief visit.

Rebecca had walked with him as he left. Aware of the tension between them. The past might always be there, pushing them apart. If she allowed it.

She didn't want the distance. She would forgive him. She could probably even say the words now, but the actual process, letting go of the pain he'd caused, would take longer. But it would do him good to know his granddaughter.

And Allie, because Rebecca kept the most painful details from her daughter, might know a kinder version of Don Barnes, and never know the truly horrible things he'd said in the past.

She passed by a room designated for physical therapy and consultations. The door was open but the lights were off. She heard someone speaking, so she glanced inside. And spotted Isaac. He'd found a mat in a corner and was stretched out, still in his boots, with his cowboy hat tossed on the floor next to him.

The horses. She wondered who had taken them all home the previous evening. Probably Joe and some of the other men—and women—from the ranch.

Isaac thrashed about on the mat, obviously having a nightmare. She approached cautiously and heard him mutter something about the child. The girl. She knelt next to him, lightly touching his arm. Somewhere down the hall a door banged.

Like a bolt, he shot off the floor, knocking her back

in the process. His eyes were wild and he didn't seem to notice her. She pulled back, unhurt but frightened. Not for herself, but for him.

"Isaac, wake up. The little girl is okay. Allie is okay." She had a feeling Allie wasn't the child in his dreams. But maybe if he heard her, it would change the dream. It was worth a shot.

"She's fine because you were there."

He closed his eyes tight, opened them again. Then he saw her on the floor. He dropped to his knees in front of her. "Did I hurt you?"

His hands touched her face, as if searching for injuries.

"I'm fine. You didn't hurt me. What are the dreams about?"

He sat back against the wall and drew her to his side. "Isaac?"

He sighed. "Afghanistan."

"When you were injured?"

"There was a little girl. We all kind of adopted her. I'm sure she had parents, but she was poor. So many poor people there. She would catch us working and want to try to speak English. We gave her fruit, bought her a doll."

"And?"

He reached for his hat, pushing it down tight on his head. "She was there the day of the explosion. She took off down the street."

"Stop." Rebecca reached for his hand. "You don't know what happened to her. She might have made it. Maybe she was already past the area when the explosion went off."

"I don't know."

"Maybe she's somewhere growing up. Maybe she has a boyfriend. Or her parents have moved."

He grinned and leaned against her just a bit. "Yeah, maybe. I'll try to keep that thought."

Rebecca stood, reached for his hand and pulled him to his feet. But the movement brought them close together and that brought back memories of being in his arms. He touched his forehead to hers.

"I don't want to hurt you, Rebecca. Ever."

"Trust. Isn't that what you told me when you put Allie on the back of the horse? I trust you." She had known this man less than a month, but he needed to know. "I trust you."

She trusted him with her life. With her heart. But she didn't trust him to accept it if she told him all that.

"Don't." His forehead was still lightly touching hers and his hands moved, one sliding beneath her jaw as he tipped her face, giving him access to her mouth. He kissed her gently, slowly, taking her heart piece by piece.

"No," he said, as he backed away from her. "Because you'll give me all of that trust and I can't promise you anything. I won't be responsible for hurting you. I won't put a woman or child through the same painful existence me or my siblings lived through. If you don't believe me, ask Carson about the night his mother took them and left."

"I don't need to ask Carson. Jack has shared his stories with me. I also know that you're not Jack. You have to trust yourself, Isaac. That might be more important than my trust."

"Maybe. And maybe I'm a fool."

She glared at him.

A glimmer of amusement flickered in the depths of

his eyes and then was gone. "Okay, we both know I'm a fool. And I want to know that we're friends. I want to be there when Allie rides in her first horse show. Or breaks every state record in barrel racing."

"As my friend."

He shrugged. "As your friend."

She left him standing there. Because she didn't want to lose her friend. She also didn't want to lose her heart. Maybe it was too late for that. She also didn't want to lose herself. She had never pleaded for a man to give her a chance. She wouldn't start now.

The difference was, this man was worth taking a chance with. And he didn't even know it. He didn't realize there were far greater ways to hurt a woman than by accident as he was having a PTSD-induced nightmare.

A police officer was waiting outside Allie's room. When she saw him, her heart froze. She hurried forward.

"Allie?" She tried to get past him.

"Miss Rebecca Barnes?" He stopped her. "I need to talk to you."

"My daughter? Is she okay?"

"What's going on?" Isaac called out.

She spun to face him as her mom walked out of the room. "What is going on out here?" she asked.

"Miss Barnes, I'm investigating a possible break-in. Do you have a salon on Lakeside Drive in Hope?"

"My daughter is okay?"

He gave her a look that clearly said he thought she'd lost it. "Yes, your daughter is fine. I'm here because the local officer was patrolling this morning and noticed the door open. When the officer went inside, he found that your shop had been burglarized."

"Greg," she said. "I can't believe this. I just opened the business."

"We'll go check things out." Isaac stepped forward, showing that she could trust him. Even if he didn't trust himself.

"What am I going to do?"

"One thing at a time," he told her.

The officer cleared his throat. "I'm afraid the damage is extensive. And I'll need for you to take inventory of what might have been stolen."

"Of course." She slid a hand over her eyes, but forced herself, for Allie's sake, to pull herself together.

"We'll head that way as soon as possible," Isaac told the officer. "And thank you for coming over here."

"No problem. You said the name Greg? Is that someone you suspect might have done this?"

"Yes, Greg Baxter. I filed a report a week ago. He met me at my shop and was physically abusive. He wanted money and threatened me. Last night he approached my daughter—*his* daughter—at the parade in Hope."

"Miss Barnes, I would encourage you to get a restraining order until we can catch this man. I'll see if I can find something in our records so we have a photo of him, and we'll issue a BOLO so that all officers in the area are looking for him."

"I appreciate that."

He told them all goodbye and left.

"What will I do? How can I make a business work if I've already lost my inventory and furnishings?"

"Let's wait until you see the damage. Don't automatically assume the worst," Isaac answered.

"You're right." Of course he was right. She gathered her composure and stepped inside Allie's room. "Hey, kiddo, I think they're going to do a few tests and then we'll go home."

Allie remained focused on the television. "Why was the policeman here? Was it about last night?"

"Partially. I'm going to pack up your stuff so when you get back we will be ready to go. Where are your shoes?"

"Nana has them," Allie said with a big grin. *Nana.* Of course, every kid wanted one of those. The word meant warm hugs, cookies, someone to teach her to knit and to share secrets with.

Greg could take a lot from them, but he couldn't take away this relationship between Allie and her nana.

Three hours later Rebecca realized that Greg could take her dreams. As she stood in the center of her salon with the police officer, Jack and Isaac, she realized that all the times in her life that she thought she'd been overwhelmed, she hadn't been. Not at all.

This was overwhelming. Not only had Greg trashed her shop, he'd stolen from her. He'd stolen merchandise, trust, dreams and her future.

"I'm done." She walked away from the group, touching the empty clothes rack. He'd stolen the clothing. He'd stolen hair products. He'd taken the jewelry she'd purchased from a local crafter.

"You're not done." Isaac spoke as he got closer to her. "You have friends."

"Yes, but this isn't something a friend can fix. Christmas is coming up. I just don't know what we'll do." For the second time someone had come in—once through a door left open, and this time a locked door—and had stolen from her.

"I keep thinking, enough. Enough of this pain. Enough feeling like I'm being punished. Just enough."

"There's a verse—"

She held up a hand. "Please, not the one about God not giving me more than I can handle. I know. I really do know. I know I can keep moving forward. I know this isn't the end of the world and I can get another job. I still have Allie. I have what's important."

"I was going to say—" he winked as he spoke "—that God promised to give you the desires of your heart. This is your dream, so don't let a man take it away from you. Tribulations produce perseverance. Don't give up."

"Perseverance produces character and character produces hope. Right?"

He kissed her forehead. Her heart broke a little, because she might persevere, but she would miss him in the process.

Wednesday morning, Isaac woke up early. He moved hay for cattle and bad-mouthed the meteorologist who had said something about a light snow. It was too early in the month for snow. When he came out of the barn, Rebecca's car was still parked in front of the apartment. If she wasn't going to be proactive in the perseverance department, he would have to help her.

That's what friends did for one another.

He found Jack in the family room of the main house. He had his feet up and was reading the Bible. Isaac stood for a moment in the doorway, unnoticed. Jack had gone through a lot, but this man, the one Isaac looked up to, admired, loved, this was a father to be proud of.

"What do you want?" he asked, without looking to see that it was Isaac at the door.

"Sorry. Didn't want to disturb you." Isaac entered the sun-soaked room. Not a cloud in the sky. He hoped that meant the forecast was wrong. He could do without the cold.

"You're not disturbing me. I'm resting. I got up this morning and went out to check on the new mare. I think she's going to foal soon. It'll be a Christmas surprise, because that guy we bought her from said he didn't know she was pregnant. Said he had her in a field with other mares. I don't think this is a miracle by any means, and I don't want to imply he's lying but we'll probably end up with a mule or something half-Shetland. I've never liked those ponies."

"I know. Where's Maria?"

"She's mad at me." He humphed and went back to reading his Bible.

"You know she loves you, right?"

Jack's gaze came up. "Don't be ridiculous. She's still in love with her husband. Passed away about thirty years ago."

"She loves you. I'm just saying, it's worth taking a chance."

"Is it?" Jack sat up and put his feet down. "That's quite a statement from you, considering."

"Considering what?"

"Considering you've been moping around here like someone took your favorite kitten."

"I don't like cats."

Jack pointed a shaky finger at him. "But you do like Rebecca Barnes."

"She's a good person."

"Right. So why are you bothering me again?"

Conversations like this never went well for Isaac. Jack had a way of turning things around and winning. Every time. "I came to see if I could borrow your key to Rebecca's shop."

"And why would you need to do that?"

"Because I want to surprise her. I know she hasn't had the heart to go back inside. I thought if I got the place cleaned up, it might be easier on her."

"That's mighty nice of you. The key is in my office, in the top drawer of my desk. It's got a tag on it with the name."

"Thanks. Dad."

Jack pushed a hand through his hair. "Now who is being unfair?"

"You are my dad, right?"

"Yeah, I am. I haven't been the best father to any of you, but I sure love you all."

"I haven't said it often enough, how much it means to me that you took me in. And that you came looking for me after…" He pointed to his head.

"What else would I have done? You're my son."

"Yeah, I know. I'm just used to calling you Jack."

"You can call me whatever you want, as long as you know how I feel."

"Good. And you might want to tell Maria how you feel. If she's mad at you, maybe it's because you've been blind to what is right in front of you."

Jack waved him away. "Don't get pushy. Go do your good deed and work out your own life."

"Yep."

Fifteen minutes later Isaac walked through the door of the salon. The tree Rebecca and Allie had decorated had been tossed and the decorations scattered or busted. A week until Christmas. Surely he could get this place looking like something in that amount of time. It needed to be cleaned, a chair or two replaced, and her inventory reordered. If she kept her records in the office, that would be the place to start. No matter what he did inside the building, it wouldn't matter if she didn't have inventory.

It didn't take him long to find what he needed. Shipping information with names of suppliers, phone numbers and even a packing list with the items. He made a few phone calls, asked for duplicate shipments and paid for expedited shipping.

With that accomplished, he needed a broom, dustpan and trash bags. He found a box for the broken pieces of mirrors, furniture and Christmas decorations, and started to work.

The front door chimed and Mattie walked in. She shook her head as she surveyed the damage.

"Your aunt Lola is right behind me. I saw your truck and hoped I'd find you cleaning this mess up."

"I thought if I got it started, she wouldn't feel so overwhelmed." He grabbed up some ripped towels that had been left in a pile.

"What kind of man does this to the woman who fathered his child?" Mattie pursed her lips. "If you don't want to be a dad or a husband, fine and dandy, but you can still be a man."

"I hope you aren't talking about me?" Isaac picked up another handful of trash and dumped it in the box.

"You know I'm not. I just get so aggravated. I heard some young man at the store bad-mouthing a girl he got pregnant. By golly, he's having a baby with that girl. He should at least respect her."

"Calm down, Mattie." Aunt Lola walked through the door. "You'll get your blood pressure up again and then what good will you be?"

"I haven't ever had high blood pressure, Lola."

"Maybe not, but you have a big old soapbox."

"Yeah, well, there's a ton of dirty laundry that needs to be dealt with."

Isaac had been minding his own business, doing a good deed, and now this. He held a hand up to stop the fussing. "Ladies, are you here to help me or help drive me crazy?"

"Are we making you dizzy?" Aunt Lola looked truly concerned.

"A little," he told her. "Mattie, if you would like to finish sweeping, I'll get the paint and deal with the marks he made on the wall."

"What can I do?" Aunt Lola asked. "I could write her a check."

That was the main reason she'd made him her power of attorney a year or so ago. Because she didn't mind writing people checks. And some people didn't mind taking advantage.

"No, Aunt Lola, we don't need a check."

"I can wash windows."

He led her to the back room, where they found window cleaner and paper towels. "Go with God."

She patted his cheek and headed off, singing an old hymn about when the battle was over.

"We shall wear a crown. Yes, we shall wear a crown," Mattie piped in with the chorus.

Isaac couldn't help but smile. It was the first time since Sunday that he'd truly felt like doing so. He might have put Rebecca in the friend category when he'd clearly like her elsewhere. But he could do this for her. He could make sure she knew that her dream was still intact.

He could hope, selfishly, that she didn't give up and leave town.

He wasn't sure he could handle that.

Chapter Fifteen

Wednesday evening, Rebecca went to church. She'd wanted to stay at the ranch, where she would continue to lick her wounds, but Allie had insisted on going. After all, she had Christmas play practice. And she was still going to be in the program. "Right, Mom? Right?" she'd asked. More than once.

So they were at church, and Rebecca smiled as the many friends she'd made in Hope came up to tell her how sorry they were that this had happened to her. "This" meaning the destruction of her salon. Somehow she smiled and managed to tell them that she would be fine. She'd figure something out. She just didn't know what. Not yet.

She stood at the back of the church sanctuary and watched as Allie went through her lines. Rebecca waited, holding her breath, for the song the angels sang together. Her heart stilled, finding peace for the first time in days.

Peace, my peace I give to you… She remembered learning that verse in vacation Bible school.

Kylie joined her, smiling but not saying anything.

They watched together as the adults helped the children with lines they would need to know for the program on Sunday. That put Christmas just one week away.

She didn't have plans for Christmas. She'd imagined it would be just like the previous year—Rebecca and Allie spending a quiet day alone. Last year they'd opened a few gifts, ate a baked ham, then watched movies. This year would be different. She realized that now. Being here, at Mercy Ranch, close to her parents, things would be different. For Allie's sake she wanted the change.

She still had to Christmas shop. Allie had given her a list. A small list with the usual suspects: dolls, craft items, a certain pair of shoes that she loved. And at the top of the list was a note to please make sure she was in Hope on Sunday for the program. Of course they would be. It was important to Allie. That made it important to Rebecca.

"Will you spend Christmas with your parents?" Kylie asked, as the kids were heading to the back of the church to remove their costumes. Allie's costume had been cleaned and new wings had been found to replace the pair that had been crumpled.

"They haven't said anything. I'm not sure. I thought I might go to Grove and look for a job. I'm going to need an income soon."

"What about your salon here?" Kylie asked.

"I don't have the money to replace everything Greg destroyed. He probably sold all of my supplies."

"Are they any closer to finding him?"

"They say they have leads. And of course they're watching for him. They have extra patrols around town, just in case he shows up again." She felt better knowing that. "Really, I just hope he's long gone."

Kylie wrapped an arm around her shoulders and pulled her close. "I'm sure you do. Just getting back to normal would be nice. And I'm hoping you are able to make things work for you here in Hope. We really do love having you all here."

"I'll just have to figure out a way to earn the money to make repairs. Jack and I had a deal, and I don't want him to be hurt by this. He wants to fill the buildings with businesses for the sake of the town, and I'm not sure when I'll be able to open back up."

"Well, let's just pray about that."

Aunt Lola walked by as they were talking. She stopped to stare at them, as if trying to place them, and then she smiled.

"Hi, Aunt Lola," Kylie greeted the older woman. "Did Isaac bring you to church?"

"Nope, Mattie did. We worked all afternoon." She turned to Rebecca. "My goodness, girl, you need to learn to clean house. That place was a mess. But I think we've got it almost livable."

Kylie and Rebecca both had no clue what she was talking about.

"You must have me mistaken for someone else," Rebecca said. "I don't have a house here."

"That place of yours downtown. It was a mess. I can't imagine living that way. But to each their own. And why my nephew would want a messy housekeeper, I just don't know."

Kylie snorted and Rebecca realized it was a laugh she was trying to hold in.

"What's so funny?" Rebecca asked.

"I think she means the salon." She spoke to Aunt Lola. "Honey, do you mean the beauty shop downtown?"

"I do and it was a mess."

"You were in my salon?" Rebecca asked.

Lola sighed. "How else could a woman clean that place up? You're a messy one. Next time try a trash can and a little ammonia."

"I'll try to remember that."

Isaac's aunt wandered off, still mumbling about the younger generation.

"Should I know what that was about?" Rebecca asked.

"I can only guess that she was inside the salon today."

"I thought Jack and I were the only ones with keys."

Kylie arched a brow and shrugged. "I couldn't say."

"Couldn't or wouldn't?" Rebecca stopped questioning her, because Allie was approaching. She was talking to a friend and Jersey walked next to her.

Despite all the upheaval lately, it still felt good to be here. Rebecca wouldn't undo what she'd done. She wouldn't return to Arizona. She wouldn't want to go back to the ten years of estrangement from her parents. She might never understand their actions, but forgiving them had started a healing process she hadn't expected.

"I think we should go check out your shop," Kylie suggested.

"Good idea." Because now she was definitely curious.

She followed Kylie out of the building, and from the parking lot she could see Lakeside Drive and her shop. The lights were on and there were cars parked out front. She motioned for Allie to get in the back seat of the car.

Rebecca didn't trust herself to speak, not with her heart in her throat the way it was.

They drove to the salon in blessed silence, with Allie refraining from even having a conversation with Jersey. Rebecca parked in front of the grocery store. Her phone rang and the caller ID said Private.

"Allie, I'm going to step out of the car. You wait here." She got out and answered the phone. "Hello."

"Hi, beautiful Becca." Greg's voice made her skin crawl. "How's my little girl doing? You know what upsets me is that you won't make this easy and just hand over the money. The stuff inside your shop didn't bring much. That means we have to bargain. Allie and her dog, or the money."

From across the street she made eye contact with Kylie. Rebecca kept herself from looking around, but she knew he had to be out there somewhere. She smiled into the car at Allie, wanting her to be reassured. She could tell by the look on her daughter's face that the smile wasn't reassuring.

"I would love to help you out. Unfortunately, I've had some unexpected expenses." She tapped on the car. "Allie, let's go inside."

"You're spineless." He laughed after delivering the insult. "So is your boyfriend, if I ever get ahold of him."

"Not my boyfriend," she whispered. "After you, I'm happier being single."

She opened the back door and Allie got out. Rebecca reached for her hand and gripped it tightly. She nodded toward the salon, where she could see people gathered. Isaac was on his phone and Kylie stood in front of him, watching Rebecca.

"Where you going, Becca?"

"Inside. With my friends."

"Sweet."

As she walked, she heard a motor rev. She glanced in the direction of the café parking lot. Tires squealed as a car took off.

"Run, Allie." They were almost to the sidewalk when Greg came roaring up the street in their direction. And just as he hit the intersection, a police car flew past, blocking his way. He slammed on his brakes and the car turned sideways, barely missing the cruiser.

A strong hand grabbed her arm and pulled her forward. "Rebecca, move."

She nodded, allowing Isaac to lead her inside. She blinked against the bright interior lights of the shop. A half-dozen people were there, all hard at work. Although the tasks seemed to be put on hold as they gathered to watch what was happening outside. All but Isaac and Kylie, who stood with Rebecca and Allie. Jack pushed up out of his chair and made his way to where they were huddled.

"They got him," someone at the front of the store called back to them.

Rebecca slumped against Isaac, thankful for his solid frame and strong arms around her. Allie tried to tug away from her.

"No," Rebecca said.

"I want to see him." Allie looked up, a pleading expression in her chocolate-brown eyes. "I need to really look at him because what if I never see him again?"

Rebecca didn't know what to say. She understood Allie's feelings. This man, vile person that he was, would always be a part of her. He was her father. He would never fill that role but still…

"They're bringing him to the window," Isaac told them. "They'll want you to identify him."

Rebecca nodded, but she still held tight to Allie. She moved her daughter forward a half-dozen feet so she could see more clearly. The police officer led the man in handcuffs to a spot on the sidewalk where the light shone down on him.

"He's kind of creepy. Are you sure you loved him?" Allie strained to get closer.

"It wasn't love," Rebecca said. "It wasn't love, but I have you. And I love you."

She nodded at the police officer. He said something to Greg and then led him off. Isaac's phone rang. He listened for a second and then hung up.

"They think he's also a suspect in an armed robbery that happened last night. If that's the case, you won't be seeing him anytime soon."

Rebecca whispered a quiet thank-you to God and then pulled her daughter close. "I'm sorry."

"Why?" Allie asked. "He's bad. That isn't our fault."

"That's very true." Rebecca hugged her close and finally allowed herself to relax. After a few minutes she glanced around the shop. "Oh, my…"

"Surprise," Isaac said, with a big grin on his face.

She looked him up and down. "You've been here all day?"

He was a mess, with dirt-stained jeans and paint splatters on his face, his shirt and in his hair. Her heart was so full she couldn't imagine being able to take a deep breath.

"We all were," he answered. "Holly closed early and everyone at the café came to help. How did you know?"

"Aunt Lola said I needed to learn to clean house. I'm apparently too messy for words."

He laughed. She loved that laugh, full-timbered and husky. She loved his smile, the way he included her daughter in everything, and the way he encouraged her to keep trying. She loved that he would spend a whole day making sure she had her dream.

"There's new merchandise ordered. It should be delivered by next week. And a couple new chairs."

"You shouldn't have done that."

"We have to keep you here, Rebecca. The town needs a salon. Haven't you heard? People have to drive twenty minutes to get a trim. No one wants that. And the barber's hands are shakier than Jack's."

Allie ran off to talk to Jack, who had gone back to supervising from a lawn chair in the corner. Rebecca stared up at the man standing in front of her.

She loved him.

"You're quiet," he said.

"I'm stunned. I never thought something like this would happen. And I can't tell you how much it means to me."

"We're friends. And you're a part of this community. The people here care about you and about Allie. You've had a tough time and they wanted to help make things a little easier."

And in making this happen for her, he broke her heart just a little. As she stood there contemplating how to accept his generosity and his offer of friendship, she realized she would have to move off the ranch. It was too difficult, seeing him every day, having Allie spend time with him daily, and knowing that he had real convictions about remaining single.

So Rebecca thanked him, because he'd done such a beautiful thing for her, and then made her way around the room, thanking the others who had volunteered. It was overwhelming to have so many people on her side.

It was overwhelming, after so many years of blaming herself for what people, specifically men, had done to her, to realize it was them, not her. She'd been taken advantage of. She'd been hurt. She'd been stolen from. And it hadn't been her fault.

If she learned nothing else from Isaac, she had learned that there were good, decent men in this world. And maybe, someday, she would find one who actually wanted her in his life.

Isaac spent Thursday and Friday catching up on ranch work he didn't get done on Wednesday. They had cattle to move to a field with a little more grass. He, Joe and a new guy named Ross took care of that. Ross was a decent hand. He'd grown up on a ranch in New Mexico, so he knew his way around a horse and he knew cattle.

He didn't much care for people. After moving cattle, they'd loaded steers to take to auction, then done some work with a couple of younger geldings they were training for cutting horses. On Friday evening, when Isaac walked out of the barn, he realized he hadn't seen Rebecca's car in a couple days. He thought maybe she was at her salon, but with the sun going down, he figured she'd be back soon.

He headed for the apartment complex she shared with Eve and Sierra. After a few minutes Eve opened the door. She stared at him, not saying anything.

"Is Rebecca here?"

She pushed her wheelchair forward and looked out the door. "I think you know she isn't. If she was here, you would see her car. She clearly is not here. And you clearly aren't as bright as I always gave you credit for. Now go away."

"What?"

She started to close the door. He stuck his boot in the opening to stop her.

"Go away," she repeated. She looked downright furious as she stared at him.

Like a mad little pixie.

"Come on, Eve. I'm not the enemy."

"No, you're not. You're just a man."

"Okay, I'm a man. But I would like to know that my friend is okay."

"Friend?" Eve shook her head. "Moron."

"Thanks." He leaned against the door frame. Maximus came out to keep him company. "I'm not going anywhere until you tell me where Rebecca is."

"She left. She's staying with Kylie and Carson. She thought it would be too awkward being here. She wouldn't tell me why, but I assumed you had something to do with her sudden decision to vacate the premises. And I'm not happy with you. I like Rebecca, and Allie is a kid I can handle spending time with."

"But she's staying. She isn't leaving Hope."

"Not leaving Hope, just leaving you." She gave him a catty little smirk. "I meant to say she's just leaving the ranch."

He waved goodbye as he turned and walked away. He needed to talk to Rebecca. He needed to make sure she was okay. The only way to do that was to head for Carson's place and hope she would talk to him.

When he knocked on his brother's door, he had to wait a minute for Kylie to answer. She didn't immediately invite him in. She stood there looking at him as a cat circled his legs.

"What?" he finally asked.

"It's just...you don't normally visit us here."

"Yeah, well, I..."

"I'll get her. You can talk out here."

"You're not even going to invite me in?"

She peeked back inside. "Allie is in here. I think you and Rebecca have to talk. Allie doesn't need to be included in that conversation."

"You're right. Thank you."

She closed the door. A moment later it opened again. Rebecca stepped out. She was beautiful, with her long blond hair hanging loose. She wore black pants, a long sweater and boots. Her nails were painted crimson and reminded him of Christmas. She reminded him of Christmas. He just wished he could tell her that.

"What do you need, Isaac?"

"I know this makes me sound like a typical male, but I noticed your car was gone."

She laughed briefly. "For two days?"

"I've been busy moving cattle. And I'm a typical male."

"Right."

"I hope you aren't going to leave Hope. I don't want to be the reason you go. And I don't want you to leave the ranch. Eve is pretty upset with me because you left."

Her tender smile warmed his heart, made him feel less alone. "I can't come back to the ranch. Allie loves you all and she really loves it there, but the longer we stay, the more she'll think that the ranch is her forever home. And it isn't. I can't stay there. I have to find a place that is ours. The more stability we have, the healthier she'll be. So I'm praying, trying to decide if Hope is where we stay, or if this was just our home for this season in our lives."

"Whatever you decide, I want you to know I admire everything about you. And if this was just your home for a season, I'm glad we were included."

"Me, too." She leaned forward to kiss his cheek. "I'm glad you're my friend."

"Rebecca," he began, but he didn't know what he intended to say. He noted that sadness settled in her warm brown eyes.

"Say goodbye, Isaac." She touched his hand. "I'll see you Sunday."

"Yes, Sunday."

But she wouldn't be at the ranch, sharing coffee with him in the mornings or taking sunset rides to the pond. He hadn't expected to miss her, not the way he already did.

Chapter Sixteen

"Mom, have you already bought my Christmas presents?" Allie asked as they drove to church on Sunday. "Because we don't really have our own tree this year, so I don't know where you're going to put them."

Rebecca gave her daughter a sideways look. "Of course you have gifts. I haven't wrapped them yet. Remember, you did give me a list."

"Yeah, I know."

This conversation had nothing to do with gifts. She could tell by the look on Allie's face.

"Do you think Isaac will be at the Christmas program?" Allie asked as they parked.

"Of course he will."

"Good. I miss him. And Jack. I really liked living on the ranch. Not that I don't like living at Carson and Kylie's. They've all been really nice, taking us in. Like we're homeless."

Oh, my. "Yes, they've been wonderful. You know we're not really homeless."

"We don't have a home. Isn't that being homeless?"

"True, but I'm going to rent us a home. Jack was kind

enough to give us an apartment at the ranch, but now it's time for us to get our own place."

"In Hope?"

"I don't know."

"But I like living here. I like the people and my school."

"I know and I'm praying about it. I want to be sure we're doing the right thing."

"Well, I think the right thing is to go back to the ranch."

"What is right isn't always what we want, or even what we like."

"That's messed up," Allie grumbled. "I'm sorry."

"It's okay. And you don't have to worry, you have Christmas gifts. They'll be under the tree on Christmas Day." She just didn't know what tree or where that tree would be located.

"Do you know what I'd like for Christmas?" Allie continued. "Not this Christmas, but maybe someday? I'd like a family. Like Carson, Kylie and their kids. A whole family. With a mom *and* a dad."

Rebecca squeezed her eyes closed and prayed for patience, for wisdom and that her heart wouldn't break. "Oh, Allie."

"I said the wrong thing," Allie moped.

"No, you didn't. You said a perfectly normal thing. I'm just so sorry that I haven't given you a family."

"It felt like a family when we lived at the ranch. Isaac was there. And Eve, Jack, Joe and Sierra. Not just Isaac. It's just, he's a lot like Carson. He might not be a dad, but he acts like one."

Her daughter was chatty this morning. And each word hit a target, namely, Rebecca's heart.

"I know you miss them." That was why they had to move. They had to find their own place before Allie got too attached to Isaac and the ranch.

"It's okay. Someday we'll have a family. You'll fall in love and get married, Mom. Just make sure he's nice. Like Isaac."

Rebecca nearly groaned. "Okay, time to go inside now."

They crossed the parking lot, and as they neared the church, she saw her parents waiting on the sidewalk. Allie let out a squeal and took off, Jersey running alongside her. Rebecca almost told her to slow down. But what fun would childhood be if a parent was constantly telling a child to slow down?

Rebecca's mom caught Allie in her arms and held her for a precious moment. Next it was Don Barnes's turn. He touched the back of her head, then hugged her, their first real connection. Rebecca approached, more cautious than her daughter.

"You came," she said.

"We wouldn't have missed this for anything." Her father held a hand out to her, but then changed his mind. He hugged her instead. "You've done a good job with this little girl."

"Thank you." She smiled down at Allie. "She's an angel. In the program, that is. In real life she's an amazing nine-year-old who has a lot of opinions."

"In other words, she's a lot like her mother?" Rebecca's father teased. He smiled, and she smiled back.

"Exactly like her mother. We should go inside. Allie has to get ready for her big performance."

"Before we go in…" Alice Barnes paused and looked

at her husband. "We would like for the two of you to spend Christmas with us."

Allie began to hop up and down. "Can we? Mom, can we? And then we could have our gifts under their tree. And we could have Christmas dinner at their house." Allie looked at her grandmother. "Do you bake pies?"

Alice nodded. "I do bake pies."

Rebecca met her father's eyes and nodded in turn. "We'd love to."

It was still winter, but for Rebecca it was a new season. A season of acceptance and forgiveness. She walked through the doors of the church with her parents. Allie immediately took off, waving goodbye as she headed down the hall.

"Does she need our help?" Rebecca's mother asked.

"No, they have plenty of help. They asked that the parents find seats so that they don't have too many people backstage. It's very crowded."

"I see." She looked around the sanctuary. "Where do we sit?"

Suddenly Isaac appeared at Rebecca's side. "With us, if you'd like."

Before she could answer, her father accepted for them. Isaac's hand went to the small of her back and he guided her down the aisle to the pew where Jack and Carson were sitting.

Squeezed in with both families, Rebecca tried to relax, but she kept thinking of Allie. When her daughter looked for her she would see her sitting with Isaac. Her overactive nine-year-old imagination would start to believe this was her Christmas gift. Or an answer to prayer.

"Uncomfortable?" Isaac asked.

"No, just... Allie."

"Small person, miniature of you."

"Yes, that one." She shook her head. The lights in the church dimmed, although sunshine filtered through the stained glass windows.

The story started with Mary and Joseph reading a decree that said they had to go to Bethlehem. Mary was obviously with child, although her pillow kept trying to fall and Joseph kept pushing it up. She smacked at his hand and gave him an angry look. The donkey, a boy in a costume, got tired of waiting and curled up on his side, kicking at them when they told him to get up.

Finally, the young couple headed off to Bethlehem, where the innkeeper told them he had no rooms so they were out of luck and could sleep with the sheep. Poor Mary began to cry and her pillow started to fall again.

The audience laughed, but did so quietly. After all, Mary and Joseph were young and didn't realize that their pillow baby amused all the adults who were watching the program.

"There's our angel," Isaac murmured. Mary and Joseph were silent and their side of the stage was dark. Shepherds and sheep were suddenly illuminated and angels appeared from the heavenly realm to tell them of the good tidings that would be for all people: "Today, a Savior who is Christ the Lord is born in Bethlehem."

Allie stepped forward and began to sing, "Glory to God in the highest and on Earth, peace and goodwill to men."

"Perfect." Alice spoke softly, clasping her hands together. "I'm so glad we were able to be here today."

The shepherds heeded the advice of the angel. They

rounded up their very stubborn sheep and headed off to Bethlehem.

The play lasted only another five minutes, and as Mary remembered what was told to her and pondered it all in her heart, the shepherds and angels began to sing "Away in a Manger."

The play ended. The audience clapped and the children bowed.

"There are sandwiches and desserts in the fellowship hall." Isaac stood, and when her father spoke, he had to turn his head. "I'm sorry, deaf in that ear."

Don Barnes apologized. "This is a good little church. I'm glad my daughter found you all."

Isaac winked at Rebecca. "So are we."

She needed a moment to herself. Her heart was breaking and the sound of it cracking had to be loud enough for everyone to hear.

But instead of escaping, she got tangled up in the crowd that included her parents, Isaac, Jack and several others from the ranch. Her father moved along next to Jack, the two talking as if they were old friends. Rebecca's mother stayed close to her side, with a hand on her back. Protective.

Where had she been when Rebecca's father put her on that bus to Arizona? Rebecca took a deep breath, releasing her anger. Someday soon they would sit down and have that conversation. Today was for Allie.

It wasn't about Isaac. It wasn't about the past. It was about Allie, the Christmas program and knowing that there was grace and mercy in the world today because of a baby born thousands of years ago.

She could show her father mercy. Even if it hadn't been shown to her.

* * *

Isaac spotted Rebecca in the kitchen. She was filling glasses with ice and pouring drinks. He'd already talked to Allie. She was sitting with her grandparents. She'd talked about the program and how the sheep were smelly because they were mostly little boys. And poor Mary and her pillow. He'd let her talk, and then he'd gone to find her mother.

Rebecca looked up when he approached. He took the pitcher of tea from her hand. "You're pouring it on the counter."

She looked down and gasped. He handed her a towel and she wiped up the mess. "That was clearly your fault, for startling me."

"I'm startling?"

"Yes, and not in a good way," she teased. "So why are you here, startling me?"

"I wanted to make sure you have somewhere to spend Christmas."

"We're going to my parents'. I think we'll stay with them for a while. Allie is off from school for Christmas so we have a couple of weeks to make a permanent plan."

"The shop?"

"I'm going to keep it open. After all you did to help get it put back together, I can't abandon it. I don't think I'm supposed to quit. Not yet. For now this seems to be the season to repair my relationship with my parents. So we're going to stay there in Grove and I'll drive back and forth to Hope. And Allie is going to stay in the Hope elementary school for the rest of the year."

"I'm glad to hear that." He filled a few more glasses with ice and she poured tea. "Dad has gifts for the two of you. So do I. If you get a chance to come over to the ranch before Christmas, we'd like that."

She shook her head and didn't look him in the eye. "I can't. We can't. Isaac, she asked me to get her a family for Christmas. She wants a dad. And you're the dad she wants. I don't want to give her the wrong idea, and us joining you all at the ranch for Christmas would."

"I'm sorry." He was more sorry than he could say. For a lot of reasons.

"It's not your fault. I mean, it is. You're a man any little girl would want for a father. But I have to protect her."

"I know you do. I understand. Jack will, too." He filled a few more glasses. "This is goodbye, isn't it?"

"Yeah, it is. Not really goodbye, because we'll see each other around town. I just can't be at the ranch."

"I get that." He finished and put the ice container back in the freezer. "I'll let Jack know."

"Isaac, we're going to miss you all. And the ranch," she told him. "He's meant so much to us. And so have you. I don't know what we would have done without you all."

"I'm glad we were here for you. Being dizzy that day had its upside."

"Yeah, it did."

He bent down and kissed her cheek. "I have to go find Jack and make sure he doesn't get in trouble with Maria. I think he might be courting her. Finally."

"Finally," Rebecca echoed.

He didn't go find Jack. Instead he wandered outside to get some fresh air. He was sitting on a picnic table watching the lake when someone sat down next to him. Carson.

"What?"

"Pathetic."

Isaac started to get off the table. Carson reached for his arm, preventing his escape.

"Say what it is you have to say," Isaac told his brother. "And then I'm going fishing. I haven't been in weeks."

"I'd go with you if you'd invite me."

"I want to go alone."

"Okay, then here it is. You're making a mistake letting that woman go. You've been happier since she showed up. It's like Rebecca and Allie complete you. Maybe you complete them. If you let them go, you're losing out."

"Thanks. I'll remember you told me that, since I'm too stupid to figure it out on my own."

"If you know, then why in the world are you telling her goodbye?"

"Because she deserves better. She's had a pretty rotten life for the past ten years, and every man that came along let her down. She is worth more than that. And Allie deserves better, too."

"You're planning on letting her down?"

"No, not planning on it. I know it'll happen. I know myself. I know my health issues. I know my nightmares. I know that I nearly broke Joe's jaw a couple of weeks ago. So Rebecca came along a month ago and shook things up for me. And maybe she thinks she feels something for me, but a month of knowing me isn't long enough."

Isaac was afraid to admit the truth. One month of knowing her wasn't nearly long enough for him. But that's all he would get with her. And it had been the best month of his life.

"When was the last time you had a nightmare?" Carson asked. He held out a hand, after gesturing for one of the toothpicks Isaac kept in his pocket. Isaac took out two and handed one to his brother.

The toothpicks were the crutch of a man who'd once found himself on the verge of addiction. Better a cinnamon toothpick than a narcotic that would destroy his life.

"I don't know. I guess a week or so."

He knew exactly. When Allie was in the hospital. He couldn't attribute the lack of nightmares ever since to the conversation with Rebecca, but he had to admit he'd been thinking about what she'd said. When the little girl crossed his mind, he pictured her alive. Happy. Thriving.

"How frequent are the headaches, and the dizzy spells?"

Big brothers who were doctors could be a real pain. Isaac jumped off the picnic table. "Not as often as they were a year ago. A lot less than two years ago."

"Would you say you're improving? I mean, have you ever woken up and thought your family was the enemy and chased them into the woods in the middle of the night?" Carson's voice lost its teasing tone as he got sucked back into his own past with Jack.

They stood there looking at one another, the secrets of the past between them. Isaac grabbed his brother in a fierce man-hug and then let him go just as quickly.

"I'm improving," he admitted.

"Give it some thought. You're awfully good at giving advice. You're happy telling people to pray and trust

God. Funny how we can all give advice about, but when it comes to our own lives, we hold on a little longer."

Yeah, funny how that was. And yet he didn't feel like laughing. At that moment he heard a child's laugh carrying across the lawn. He turned to watch as Rebecca and Allie left the church with her parents. They stopped to talk and then they got in their cars and left.

He ignored Carson's knowing look and headed for the back door of the church. The last thing he wanted was for his older brother to say he'd told him so.

Isaac knew what he had to do. But could he actually do it?

Chapter Seventeen

Christmas morning, Rebecca woke up in the home she grew up in, in the room that had been hers throughout her childhood. She managed to get up without waking Allie and tiptoed down the hall to find her mom placing gifts under the tree. Alice handed her a bag.

"Fill the stockings, please," she said. "And then you can help me make breakfast."

"Breakfast casserole and cinnamon rolls?" Rebecca asked.

"Of course. The cinnamon rolls are already on the counter. I just have to ice them." She stood back from the tree and smiled. "I'm so glad to have you home. I'm so glad to know my granddaughter. This is the greatest gift, this love, and having you back in our lives."

Rebecca hugged her mother. They were in the kitchen when they heard a joyful shout from the living room. Mother and daughter gave each other knowing smiles before heading there. Allie was sitting under the tree, Jersey licking her face. The sight gave Rebecca a start, but she realized Allie was just playing with her dog.

"What in the world is under our tree, Alice?" Don

Barnes asked as he entered the living room. "It's a child."

"The best gift of all," Alice told him. She went to his side and hugged him tightly. "The very best gift."

The doorbell rang. Rebecca's mother glanced at the clock and sighed. "It's only eight in the morning. Were you expecting someone?"

Rebecca's father shook his head. "Nope."

The doorbell rang again. With a sigh of her own Rebecca headed that way. She pulled it open and stared at the man standing outside. There were flurries falling and he was dressed in a canvas coat and carrying a big box of gifts. His grin was a little on the cheesy side, but his silver-gray eyes made up for it.

"Isaac!" Allie yelled from inside the house and the ecstatic greeting set the dog to barking.

"Allie..." Isaac held out his arms and she flew to him, letting him pick her up and twirl her in the air.

"What are you doing here?" she asked. "Where's Jack?"

"He's at home with Carson and Kylie. They're all on the ranch."

"Why aren't you there?" Allie pressed.

"Because I realized I hadn't given you your gifts. I couldn't have Christmas unless I gave these to you."

"Did you get something for my mom?" she asked.

"Allie, that isn't polite." Rebecca shot her a stern look.

Isaac smiled down at Allie. "I did get her a gift. And I realized she has something of mine. So we'll probably trade."

She didn't have anything of his. She had bought him

a gift, but she'd asked Kylie to give it to him. "I left your gift with Kylie. We didn't expect to see you today."

"Surprise, I'm here."

"Rebecca, let the man enter. You're letting all the cold air in." Rebecca's dad appeared at her shoulder. "Good to see you again, Isaac. You're just in time for breakfast."

"I don't want to impose and my family will be waiting for me. Actually, they told me to ask you all to come over this evening. Leftover potluck and games at the ranch."

"Can we?" Allie asked. "We could see everyone. And we could take some of Nana's candy."

"I don't know—" Rebecca started.

Isaac interrupted. "Just think about it. Don't answer yet."

"Let's have breakfast," Alice called out as she headed to the kitchen, clearly not understanding the tension radiating between her daughter and the man she'd invited into the house.

"You might as well have breakfast before you head back to the ranch," Rebecca's dad offered. "Alice does like to feed people. She cooked enough for a dozen and there's only four of us."

"Breakfast sounds good." Isaac ignored the look Rebecca shot him. Like her mother, he seemed oblivious.

She was the only one who seemed to understand that it would be devastating for Allie when he left. It would be devastating for Rebecca, too.

Because he was everything she wanted for Christmas, for the rest of her life. And he didn't trust himself enough to be that person in her life.

She loved him. Silly man.

"What was that?" he asked.

"Nothing. I didn't say anything."

He slipped an arm around her waist. "You clearly said something. I think you were bad-mouthing me."

"Probably," she admitted, as she poured herself a cup of coffee from the carafe on the dining room table. And because she was nice, she poured him one, as well.

The meal didn't take nearly long enough. Allie rushed everyone through breakfast and fed part of hers to Jersey who had found a place under the table. There were gifts to open and she was an impatient nine-year-old. Eating wasn't nearly as important as the colorful packages under the tree.

And the ones in the box that Isaac had dragged in with him were especially tempting.

"We should do the dishes." Rebecca started to clear the table.

Allie grabbed her grandfather by the hand and rushed him and Isaac from the room. She used the excuse that the gifts needed to be organized.

After they'd left, Rebecca's mom put a hand on her arm, stopping her from clearing the table. "Later." She gave Rebecca a curious look. "Are you okay?"

"I'm trying to protect Allie. She wants a dad." Rebecca took a deep breath and continued. "She wants Isaac in our lives. He's a friend but he isn't looking for a relationship."

"I'm so sorry." Her mother gave her a hug. "But he's here now."

"Because he's a friend."

"Maybe that's what he's supposed to be for now, a friend? Maybe you should allow that. He does seem like a good friend. Why shut him out completely?"

Rebecca let the words of advice sink in, and kissed her mother on the cheek. "Thank you, Mom. I think I really needed that."

"I'm glad. I know I let you down, but I'm here now. And I love you."

"I love you, too."

They joined the men and Allie in the living room. Allie had a pile of gifts in front of her. "Can I open them?"

"I think you should before you drive us crazy." Rebecca picked a couple packages out of her daughter's pile. "These are for your grandparents."

"And this one is for you." Allie tossed her a gift.

"That will break!" Rebecca's mother shrieked.

Allie looked contrite and apologized. "Can I open the ones from Isaac first?"

"Please do." Rebecca smiled at the man, who had taken a seat next to her daughter. Jersey had obviously missed him. Her head rested on his foot as she stretched out next to Allie.

Allie grabbed the big box from Isaac. "It's really heavy."

"Yep."

She grinned at him and started to slowly remove the tape from the package. Her grin turned ornery and she ripped the wrapping paper from the box.

"A saddle? Is it really a saddle or is that just the box you put a gift in?"

He looked over her head and winked at Rebecca. "It is a saddle."

"A real saddle? Like the kind you put on a real horse?"

"That's the kind."

She jumped up and threw her arms around his neck. "It's the best. And this is the best Christmas. It isn't lonely."

Noticing the tension in the air, Allie grew quiet. "Hey, Isaac, you said you had something for my mom."

"Yes, I do." He stood before Rebecca, but he glanced around the room at her daughter, her parents. "If you all don't mind, I think Rebecca and I need to take a walk."

"But it's cold out there," she protested, more than a little worried about what he wanted to tell her.

"We'll bundle up."

Isaac led her to the front door, where coats were hanging on the hall tree. "Which one is yours?"

She pointed to the red coat and he helped her put it on. She pulled gloves and a hat out of her pocket.

Together they walked out the front door. The flurries had turned to actual snow. The world seemed quiet, almost muffled. Few people were out on Christmas Day so everything was peaceful. The two of them walked hand in hand. She thought he'd have to say something eventually.

When he didn't, she stopped. "How far are we going to walk?"

"I don't know. I'm still trying to decide what to say. This was spur of the moment. I was sitting at the house with my family and I realized I couldn't do Christmas without you and Allie. I realized something else."

"What?" She faced him, wishing she could step into his embrace and just let him hold her as the snow fell.

"I realized I can't live my life without you. That part really took me by surprise. I've been doing life on my own and suddenly that's just too plain lonely."

She didn't know what to say to that, so remained silent.

"As I was contemplating being lonely and alone, I realized that you had something of mine."

"And what is that?" Her heart was starting to beat a little faster.

He leaned in, kissing her lightly once, twice and then again. The third kiss lingered.

"You have my heart. I think I gave it to you that day you offered me a ride. I think I willingly took it out and handed it over to you, and when you left the ranch, you didn't give it back."

"Corny cowboy," she whispered, kissing him back.

Rebecca was beautiful standing there in the snow, her coat red, her cheeks rosy from the cold.

"Corny, but was it effective?" he asked, as he leaned close once more.

"Maybe. Kiss me again and I'll let you know."

He did as she asked. A car driving by honked. He raised a hand to wave.

"What is it you want?" Rebecca asked. Her brown eyes grew serious. "Isaac, I'm a single mom. I have a daughter to raise and her heart matters, too. When I date, it has to matter. I don't have time to hang out, share a few kisses, and I don't have enough of me left to give just a part of myself to a relationship."

"I don't want just a part of you. I want all of you, Rebecca. I want you. I want your heart. I want the mom who is protective of her daughter. I want the woman who makes me laugh. I want to be a family. You. Me. Allie."

"What changed? I thought you couldn't offer anyone those things?"

Good questions. "I changed. I'm a veteran with PTSD. I have nightmares. Not as bad as they used to be. I worry a lot about the type of husband or father I would make, so I've carefully avoided both. I haven't dated a woman in years because I didn't plan on getting married. And then you came along and I want to date you. I want to send you flowers. I want to fight and then I want to kiss and make up."

"That's a lot of kissing."

"We could start now." He bent down, but she sidestepped.

"I have a daughter."

"Yes. Her name is Allie and I think she's about the most amazing child I've ever met. I love you. Loving you means I love your daughter. I want to be a parent to her. I want to be the dad she deserves."

Tears rolled down Rebecca's cheeks. He wiped them away and pulled her close, holding her against him.

"I need my heart back, Rebecca."

"I'm keeping it, cowboy. You're mine and I'm not letting you go."

Epilogue

Isaac glanced out the window. Snow was coming down, just as he'd predicted on Christmas a year ago, when he'd kind of proposed to Rebecca. He'd proposed a second time in May, when it was warm and the flowers were blooming. Allie had been with them and it just seemed liked the thing to do. He'd asked them to be his family, his wife and daughter. He'd also broken the news to Rebecca that he'd probably like about a half dozen more kids just like Allie.

They'd negotiated that part of the contract. He didn't mind. If it was always just the three of them, so be it.

"Why can't I go on the cruise?" Allie asked again.

She hadn't had a seizure in six months, the longest she'd ever gone without one. Carson had sent her to a specialist, who said sometimes children did outgrow seizures. Time would tell. It didn't matter what the doctor said; Jersey was at her side. A constant companion, just in case.

Thanks to Jersey, Mercy Ranch had a new ministry. They were going to donate service dogs to children with seizure disorders.

Thanks to God, Isaac had this new life that he'd never expected. It had all started when he stumbled out of the feed store and into a protective mom.

"Isaac!" Allie, now ten, punched his arm.

"Sorry, got lost in thought."

She rolled her eyes at that. "It's going to be warm where you're going."

He laughed. "You're going to get to build a snowman."

"I don't like snowmen. They're just cold."

"True." He bent to kiss the top of her head. "I love you, kid. You'll have a great time staying with Carson, Kylie and the kids."

"I love you, too." Her eyes misted a little and she punched him again. "Dad."

He grabbed her up and held her tight. "Thank you. I'm pretty happy to be your dad."

And he was going to love surprising her. She might think she was staying in Hope, but her bags were packed and in the back of the limo that would take them to the airport. She would share a room with Sierra, who had agreed to go along as a babysitter. It might not be the most conventional honeymoon, but it was theirs.

Jack stepped into the room, all decked out in his best suit. He stood straight and proud today, but his health was failing. He'd confided that he still had two children whose lives he needed to interfere with so he wasn't going anywhere anytime soon. Isaac kind of thought his dad would outlive them all.

"You ready?" Jack asked.

"Of course they're ready." Maria stepped in behind him, holding his arm.

"We're ready." Isaac held a rose out to Allie, and of

course she tucked it behind her ear. "You're supposed to carry that."

"What best man carries a rose?"

"Technically, you're my best kid."

She grinned. "Yeah, I'm kind of great."

"Come on, best man, we need to get to the front of the church. Just the way we rehearsed it. I'll walk down the aisle and wait. You come next with Jersey. Eve follows. And then Carson escorts Kylie."

"Why do you keep telling me?"

"Because I'm nervous, and if I tell you, you'll remember."

She took him by the arm and escorted him from the room.

"You'll do just fine, Dad."

Rebecca's father escorted her from her room. She'd never thought this day would happen. Never thought she'd find a man to love. A man who loved her and her daughter. She'd never thought she'd be in this place with her parents, with her dad at her side.

Forgiveness was a healing thing.

It had changed her life. It had changed her father.

"Are you ready for this?" he asked, as they watched Eve roll her chair down the aisle. Carson and Kylie went next.

After Carson and Kylie came Andy and Maggie, the ring bearer and flower girl. Maggie smiled back at her as she tossed rose petals in the air. Whatever she did, it would be perfect.

"I'm ready," Rebecca answered. "I think I've been waiting my whole life for this moment and this man."

"I'm thankful that you found him. I know I made

some serious mistakes as a father and a pastor. And as a Christian. I think you've taught me a lot more than I ever knew about my faith, about loving and showing mercy. You've shown me mercy, Rebecca."

"I love you, Dad."

"I love you, too. And I couldn't be happier for the three of you, that you found each other."

This was a season of her life that she hoped would linger awhile. For everything there was a season, and a time for every purpose under the sun.

The music faded from the love song they'd picked to be the wedding march. He led her forward from the vestibule and she made eye contact with Allie, standing next to Isaac. Her daughter stood straight and tall in her role as best man.

Isaac winked as Rebecca came down the aisle, but she saw past his charming cowboy demeanor. She knew the heart of this man she was marrying. And it was good.

He was decent and kind. He loved puppies and children.

But most of all, he loved her.

The walk down that aisle took longer than any walk should have taken. When they finally reached the front of the church, her father kissed her cheek.

"Be happy."

She teared up a little, but quickly composed herself. It was her wedding day. It was a time to laugh, not to weep.

Isaac reached for her hand and drew it up to his mouth, kissing it lightly. This wasn't part of the ceremony. She wanted to scold him, but couldn't get words past the tightness in her throat. She would be content to stand all day and look into his silver-gray eyes as he held her hand.

The minister cleared his own throat. "If the two of you would give me ten minutes of your day, I'll do this wedding thing, and you can hold hands for the next sixty years, looking lovingly into each other's eyes."

The people gathered laughed and Allie rolled her eyes.

Isaac released her hand, and true to the minister's words, ten minutes later he pronounced them husband and wife.

"You may kiss your bride," he said with a grin.

Isaac picked his bride up, swung her around and then kissed her. She clung to him, not caring that they had an audience.

This cowboy was hers. Forever.

* * * * *

If you loved this story,
pick up the first Mercy Ranch book,

Reunited with the Rancher

from bestselling author
Brenda Minton.

And don't miss these other great books
in the Bluebonnet Springs miniseries:

Second Chance Rancher
The Rancher's Christmas Bride
The Rancher's Secret Child

Available now from Love Inspired!
Find more great reads at www.LoveInspired.com

Dear Reader,

As I've spent time in Hope, Oklahoma, and at Mercy Ranch, I've gotten to know the characters and I've come to love this little town. I hope you'll enjoy your time here, as well!

From the beginning Isaac West quickly became a favorite of mine, and this book had to belong to him. Isaac has dealt with difficult times in his life and he's learned to laugh when things get tough. I think that's one of my favorite things about this hero.

Together Isaac and Rebecca learn that life has its seasons. They have cried, mourned, been angry, been broken. Now it is their time to laugh, to love, to heal.

I hope you enjoy taking the journey with them—and with me.

Brenda Minton

COURTING HER PRODIGAL HEART
Prodigal Daughters • by Mary Davis

Pregnant and abandoned by her *Englisher* boyfriend, Dori Bontrager returns home—but she's determined it'll be temporary. Can Eli Hochstetler convince her that staying by his side in their Amish community is just what she and her baby need?

MINDING THE AMISH BABY
Amish Country Courtships • by Carrie Lighte

Remaining unmarried and living alone is exactly the life Amish store clerk Tessa Fisher wants...until her landlord, Turner King, enlists her help caring for a baby left on his doorstep. As they search for the little girl's mother, Tessa begins to wish their instant family could become permanent.

A COWBOY IN SHEPHERD'S CROSSING
Shepherd's Crossing • by Ruth Logan Herne

When Jace Middleton learns he has family he never knew existed, he must give his two nieces a home. But his house needs renovations to make it baby friendly, and home designer Melonie Fitzgerald is just the woman to restore it—and his heart.

HER COWBOY'S TWIN BLESSINGS
Montana Twins • by Patricia Johns

Foreman Casey Courtright hoped to buy the ranch he works on, but he can't match Ember Reed's offer. Nevertheless, he agrees to show her around the land she'll be using as her therapy center...but only if she'll help him with the orphaned twin infant boys in his care.

BENEATH MONTANA SKIES
Mustang Ridge • by Mia Ross

Tyler Wilkens knows going home to recover from his rodeo injuries means seeing ex-girlfriend Morgan Whittaker again, but he doesn't count on learning he's a father to two six-year-old girls. Can he win back Morgan's trust and earn the title of daddy...and possibly husband?

THE RANCHER'S BABY SURPRISE
Bent Creek Blessings • by Kat Brookes

After losing her sister and brother-in-law, surrogate Hannah Sanders must suddenly prepare to be a single mother. When veterinarian Garrett Wade rescues her from a flash flood just as she goes into labor, Hannah can't help but hope the cowboy might be the perfect father for her infant.

———————————

LICNM1218

Get 4 FREE REWARDS!

We'll send you 2 FREE Books plus 2 FREE Mystery Gifts.

Love Inspired® books feature contemporary inspirational romances with Christian characters facing the challenges of life and love.

FREE Value Over $20

YES! Please send me 2 FREE Love Inspired® Romance novels and my 2 FREE mystery gifts (gifts are worth about $10 retail). After receiving them, if I don't wish to receive any more books, I can return the shipping statement marked "cancel." If I don't cancel, I will receive 6 brand-new novels every month and be billed just $5.24 for the regular-print edition or $5.74 each for the larger-print edition in the U.S., or $5.74 each for the regular-print edition or $6.24 for the larger-print edition in Canada. That's a savings of at least 13% off the cover price. It's quite a bargain! Shipping and handling is just 50¢ per book in the U.S. and 75¢ per book in Canada.* I understand that accepting the 2 free books and gifts places me under no obligation to buy anything. I can always return a shipment and cancel at any time. The free books and gifts are mine to keep no matter what I decide.

Choose one: ☐ **Love Inspired® Romance**
Regular-Print
(105/305 IDN GMY4)

☐ **Love Inspired® Romance**
Larger-Print
(122/322 IDN GMY4)

Name (please print)

Address   Apt. #

City   State/Province   Zip/Postal Code

Mail to the **Reader Service:**
IN U.S.A.: P.O. Box 1341, Buffalo, NY 14240-8531
IN CANADA: P.O. Box 603, Fort Erie, Ontario L2A 5X3

Want to try 2 free books from another series! Call 1-800-873-8635 or visit www.ReaderService.com

---

*Terms and prices subject to change without notice. Prices do not include applicable taxes. Sales tax applicable in N.Y. Canadian residents will be charged applicable taxes. Offer not valid in Quebec. This offer is limited to one order per household. Books received may not be as shown. Not valid for current subscribers to Love Inspired Romance books. All orders subject to approval. Credit or debit balances in a customer's account(s) may be offset by any other outstanding balance owed by or to the customer. Please allow 4 to 6 weeks for delivery. Offer available while quantities last.

Your Privacy—The Reader Service is committed to protecting your privacy. Our Privacy Policy is available online at www.ReaderService.com or upon request from the Reader Service. We make a portion of our mailing list available to reputable third parties that offer products we believe may interest you. If you prefer that we not exchange your name with third parties, or if you wish to clarify or modify your communication preferences, please visit us at www.ReaderService.com/consumerchoice or write to us at Reader Service Preference Service, P.O. Box 9062, Buffalo, NY 14240-9062. Include your complete name and address.

LI19

SPECIAL EXCERPT FROM

Love Inspired®

Pregnant and abandoned by her Englisher *boyfriend, Dori Bontrager returns home—but she's determined it'll be temporary. Can Eli Hochstetler convince her that staying by his side in their Amish community is just what she and her baby need?*

Read on for a sneak preview of
Courting Her Prodigal Heart *by Mary Davis, available January 2019 from Love Inspired!*

Rainbow Girl stepped into his field of vision from the kitchen area. *"Hallo."*

Eli's insides did funny things at the sight of her.

"Did you need something?"

He cleared his throat. "I came for a drink of water."

"Come on in." She pulled a glass out of the cupboard, filled it at the sink and handed it to him.

"Danki."

She gifted him with a smile. *"Bitte.* How's it going out there?"

He smiled back. "Fine." He gulped half the glass, then slowed down to sips. No sense rushing.

After a minute, she folded her arms. "Go ahead. Ask your question."

"What?"

"You obviously want to ask me something. What is it? Why do I color my hair all different colors? Why do I dress like this? Why did I leave? What is it?"

She posed all *gut* questions, but not the one he needed an answer to. A question that was no business of his to ask.

"Go ahead. Ask. I don't mind." Very un-Amish, but she'd offered. *Ne*, insisted.

He cleared his throat. "Are you going to stay?"

She stared for a moment, then looked away. Obviously not the question she'd expected, nor one she wanted to answer.

He'd made her uncomfortable. He never should have asked. What if she said *ne*? Did he want her to say *ja*? "You don't have to tell me." He didn't want to know anymore.

She pinned him with her steady brown gaze. "I don't know. I don't want to, but I'm sort of in a bind at the moment."

Maybe for the reason she'd been so sad the other day, which had made him feel sympathy for her.

He appreciated her honesty. "Then why does our bishop think you are?"

"He's hoping I do."

His heart tightened. "Why are you giving him false hope?" Why was she giving Eli false hope?

"I'm not. I've told him this is temporary. He won't listen. Maybe you could convince him to stop this foolishness—" she waved her hand toward where the building activity was going on "—before it's too late."

He chuckled. "You don't tell the bishop what to do. *He* tells you."

He really should head back outside to help the others. Instead, he filled his glass again and leaned against the counter. He studied her over the rim of his glass. Did he want Rainbow Girl to stay? She'd certainly turned things upside down around here. Turned him upside down. Instead of working in his forge—where he most enjoyed spending time—he was here, and gladly so. He preferred working with iron rather than wood, but today, carpentry strangely held more appeal.

Time to get back to work. He guzzled the rest of his water and set the glass in the sink. *"Danki."* As he turned to leave, something on the table caught his attention. The door knocker he'd made years ago for Dorcas—Rainbow Girl—ne, Dorcas, but now Rainbow Girl had it. They were the same person, but not the same. He crossed to the table and picked up his handiwork. "You kept this?"

She came up next to him. *"Ja.* I liked having a reminder of…"

"Of what?" Dare he hope him?

She stared at him. "Of…my life growing up here."

That was probably a better answer. He didn't need to be thinking of her as anything more than a lost *Englisher*.

Don't miss Courting Her Prodigal Heart *by Mary Davis, available January 2019 wherever Love Inspired® books and ebooks are sold.*

www.LoveInspired.com

LIEXP1218